Silence.

There wasn't a dial to ████████████ ███ down, and the panic started to ████ ██ again.

He rushed outside and yelled: ''Is there anyone down there? Anyone at all?''

There was no reply. When his voice died down, there was only silence, save for the creaking of the trees.

Nick fell to his knees on the lawn and stared all around in disbelief, shock, and fear.

Nobody. Nobody here at all but him.

Where was everyone?

Was he the last person still left in Massapequa?

Or—the horrible thought started to batter at his frightened mind—was he the last person *anywhere*? Had something terrible happened, stranding him here, all alone?

What was going on? Was there anyone else? Anyone else left at all?

The Outer Limits™

A whole new dimension in
adventure . . .

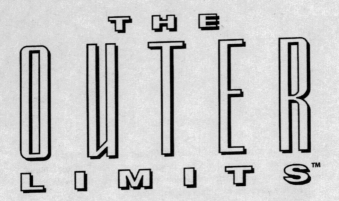

THE OUTER LIMITS™

THE VANISHED

JOHN PEEL

Tor Kids!

A TOM DOHERTY ASSOCIATES BOOK
NEW YORK

This is a work of fiction. All the characters and events portrayed in this book are either products of the author's imagination or are used fictitiously.

THE OUTER LIMITS #7: THE VANISHED

TM & © 1998 Metro-Goldwyn-Mayer Studios Inc. All rights reserved. The Outer Limits is a trademark of Metro-Goldwyn-Mayer Studios Inc., and is licensed by MGM Consumer Products.

A Tor Book
Published by Tom Doherty Associates, Inc.
175 Fifth Avenue
New York, NY 10010

Tor® is a registered trademark of Tom Doherty Associates, Inc.

ISBN: 0-812-57564-4

First edition: October 1998

Printed in the United States of America

0 9 8 7 6 5 4 3 2 1

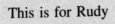

This is for Rudy

There are many elements that make up our worlds. There is the physical world itself, to begin with. Add to that the trappings of civilization—the houses, roads, churches, factories, cities. Then there are all of the people we interact with each day—parents, siblings, co-workers, classmates, teachers, bosses, friends, and lovers. Our world is thus a many-layered and often complicated process.

But what would happen if the world as we know it no longer existed? If all of the things we love, or hate, or fear, or desire—everything that we simply take for granted—were to no longer exist? If some catastrophe wiped out everything that we knew but ourselves? How then would we cope?

Would we be able to cope?

A man shipwrecked on a desert island may be desperately alone, but he knows that there is some chance of rescue. He knows that, while he is alone in his island prison, there are other people elsewhere. He is not alone in the world. This helps him to cope.

But . . . what if he were all alone in the world? If there was nobody else? And no chance of rescue?

Then what would happen?

CHAPTER 1

SILENCE.

AT FIRST it simply puzzled Nick Morganthau. Then it worried him. Finally, it scared him.

When he awoke, he frowned. Daylight was streaming into his room, and that was odd. His alarm should have gone off at six to get him up for school, and it would hardly be this bright at six . . . He rolled over and looked at his clock.

Three-thirty . . .

That didn't make sense. It wouldn't be this bright at three-thirty in the morning. And there was no way his parents would have let him sleep this long on a school day! He blinked, rubbed the sleep from his eyes, and sat up. It was definitely later than six. His alarm must have stopped working. But how come nobody had come to throw him out of bed?

Come to think of it, how come he couldn't hear his parents getting ready for work? Surely they'd be up and active even if they'd let him sleep for some reason? And what about his sister, Briony? That little brat was a bundle of energy and noise. She'd just *love* bouncing on his bed to get him up—if she wasn't running about the house making enough noise to wake the dead.

So why was it so quiet?

Nick reached over and shook the electric alarm clock. Then he listened to it. Damn! It *had* stopped! He was going to be in trouble for sure! He jumped out of bed, scratched his bare chest, and headed for the bathroom. There wasn't much chance he'd get to use it, since his folks and Briony had to be up by now, but he had to go pretty badly.

To his amazement, nobody had staked claim to it yet. He locked the door, fast, to make sure nobody would. Maybe the power had gone out in the night, and everybody's alarms had died. Was he, wonder of wonders, the first one up? If he was, he'd better wake the others, as soon as he was done in here.

He flushed the toilet, and winced at the odd sucking noise. He glanced down and saw that there was no water flowing in. That was odd. He listened, but as soon as the flushing had died, there was no sound of water running. That was malfunctioning, too. This wasn't the best of starts to the day.

Well, that was Dad's job; let him worry about it. Nick

wandered to the sink and turned on the faucets.

Nothing.

He stared at the dry sink, confused. The water supply was out, too? How come? It didn't make any sense. What would stop the water flowing? A break in the mains somewhere, maybe? This was weird. Still, it meant he didn't have to take a shower this morning, at least. On the other hand, he wouldn't mind being able to clean his teeth. They felt rather gross.

But he'd better let his parents know there was a problem or two—and get them up so they could be on their way to work. He padded down the hallway to his parents' bedroom and rapped hard on the door.

"Come on!" he yelled, enjoying the reversal of roles for once. "Can't sleep all day, you know! You've got to get up and get moving." He grinned, his ear to the door, as he waited for groans, yawns, and probably muffled curses. After a silent moment, though, he was forced to hammer on the door and howl: "WAKE UP!!!"

Nothing.

Nick was starting to get really worried now. It was a family rule that when a bedroom door was closed you didn't go in without an express invitation. But this seemed to be the time to break a rule like that. Why weren't his folks waking up? He had a sudden, dreadful image of them both in bed, dead—massacred by some silent gunman, or just dead of one of those things like heart attacks or strokes that affected older people. He really didn't want to see anything like that, but he had to *know*. Nervously he gripped the handle, steeled himself, and then pushed open the door.

He was half hoping his father would yell at him for breaking the rules.

Silence.

Nick stared into the room. Light spilled across the empty bed from the blinds. The bed was messed, and there were two sets of pajamas scattered on the floor. His folks had been there, but they certainly weren't in bed right now.

What was going on? This wasn't making any sense. If his parents had woken and got ready for work, they would certainly have never left him sleeping. And they weren't in bed . . . He went to the bed, feeling kind of foolish, and felt the depression where his mother usually slept. It was cold, so she hadn't been there for a while. So—what had happened?

Nick whirled around and went to Briony's room. "Hey, brat!" he yelled, hammering on the door. "Get moving!" He waited for a scream, curses, anything . . . but again, all he got was silence. He pushed open the door, once more seeing only an empty bed and nightclothes on the floor.

Briony was missing, too . . .

Nick was starting to get scared. Okay, Briony would happily go off to school and leave him sleeping, so he'd get into trouble. But Mom would *never* leave him. This felt really wrong. He ran to his room and threw on the first clothes he came across, lacing his sneakers fast. Then he hurried downstairs.

There was nobody there, either. The living room was empty, and the kitchen showed no signs of the usual post-breakfast disaster. No dishes, no food out, no brewed coffee. Of course, with the power out, there wouldn't be any coffee. No sign that Mom, Dad, or Briony had been here. Opening the door to the garage, Nick went inside, clicking on the light. *Shoot*, he remembered. No power.

Dad's Taurus and Mom's Silhouette were both there. So was Briony's bike.

Ice was forming around the base of Nick's spine now.

What on earth could have made his family get up, ignore him, breakfast, and the bathroom, and leave their cars and just . . . *go*? The knot of ice was crawling up his spine now.

He walked back into the kitchen as if in a trance. He was scared. This was getting to be too much. Nick couldn't make any sense out of it. His stomach growled, reminding him that he hadn't eaten yet. He opened the fridge, without the usual waft of cold air or the light coming on. Grabbing the juice, he drank some straight from the carton. Then he grabbed an apple and bit into it. At least the juice and apple, even if not cold, tasted normal.

Munching on the apple, Nick went to the front door. He suddenly realized that he hadn't heard so much as a sound since he'd woken that he hadn't made. He hesitated, his hand on the doorknob, and listened. There was no sound of passing cars; no kids laughing and yelling; no radios blaring; not even any birds singing or dogs barking.

Nothing but the soft sound of wind through branches.

It was downright spooky.

Nick had to force himself to open the door and walk outside. He was overcome by an odd sensation: it felt like he was leaving his only protection. The door clicked closed behind him and he grabbed for the key in his pocket. Sighing with relief, he kidded himself. "Easy, Nick," he said. "This is no time to go wacko." He forced himself to focus on the task at hand.

Where *was* everybody? His family couldn't have just vanished overnight. Those sorts of things didn't happen. He needed to find somebody in authority, like a cop, and get some inquiries started. File a missing persons report or something.

Except there was a huge flaw in this plan.

Nick walked slowly toward the road, searching in both directions. Massapequa was normally a busy town, with Sunrise Highway only about half a mile south. It didn't matter what time of the day it was, there were always plenty of cars around—heading for school, work, play, or the mall, or just passing through on the way to points east or west. There were cars even in the dark hours of the early morning. There were *always* cars.

Except today.

There was nothing moving beyond a few tree boughs sighing in the wind. No cars, no bikes, no *people* even. Not a dog or a cat on the prowl. Not a bird or a butterfly on the wing.

Nothing—except Nick. He glanced into the sky. Not even a passing aircraft, and that was another thing that there always was.

The sky was clear, except for scuttling clouds like ducklings running for their mother. The road was clear, too, except for a few parked and empty cars. And the houses looked as silent and dead as so many tombs.

This was getting way beyond *spooky* and right up there into *terrifying*. Nick had never liked things too quiet, but he'd never known how quiet things could get before this moment. There was nothing around . . . but him.

Panicking slightly, he ran next door to the Howards. He hammered on the front door. No answer. "Crap!" muttered Nick. He ran around to the side door, which was hardly ever locked. It was open now. He went inside, and called out for someone—anyone—to answer. Nobody did. He checked the downstairs rooms, then rushed upstairs. The beds had been slept in. He found nightclothes discarded on the floor and over chairs. "Charlie!" shouted Nick. Charlie, the Howard's big Labrador, would normally have been all over Nick by now. "Charlie!"

Charlie was gone, too.

Slowly Nick retreated to the living room. "OK. OK. OK," he said out loud, calming himself. There had to be a logical explanation, right? It was impossible that his family had vanished. It was even more impossible that the neighbors had, too. For God's sake, where could they have all gone to? And without waking him? What possible disaster could have occurred to leave him stranded here like this?

And *how* had all of the people left? Their cars were still here. They couldn't all just have walked off, could they? He had a sudden image of hundreds of sleepwalkers, arms outstretched, marching off into . . . what? Then he discarded the idea. After all, he'd seen the nightclothes on the floor. They could hardly have all marched off butt-naked. And he didn't think that a legion of zombies would take the time to get dressed first. They must have been conscious and aware of what they were doing when they left.

But *why* would they go? And more important, why would they leave him behind? If there had been some emergency—like a meltdown at a nuclear plant or something—not even Briony would be so cruel as to leave him sleeping while everyone fled.

Besides, *how* had they fled? The cars were still here. And granted, he wasn't a light sleeper, but if the whole neighborhood had woken up in the night and left for some reason, surely *something* would have wakened him?

He had to find someone in authority, and then he'd get some information. Even if everyone had been evacuated for some reason, there were bound to be some cops left behind to collect stragglers like himself. He just had to find a cop, that was all.

Nick laughed, nervously. He didn't have a clue where the nearest police station was. He'd never had any run-ins with the law, which suited him just fine. But now he realized how ignorant he was. Where would the police precinct be?

He glanced at the phone and grinned at last. Even if the power and water were out, the phones should work. They were on separate lines. All he had to do was call 911 and he'd connect to the operator. Then he'd find out something. Feeling relieved, he scooped up the receiver and listened for the dial tone, his finger poised to push buttons.

Silence.

There wasn't a dial tone. There wasn't anything. He rattled the phone, tapped at the buttons, and then cursed. Nothing made a sound. He slammed the receiver down, and the panic started to close in again.

He rushed outside and yelled: "Is there anyone there? Anyone at all?"

There was no reply. When his voice died down, there was only silence, save for the creaking of the trees.

Nick fell to his knees on the lawn and stared all around in disbelief, shock, and fear.

Nobody. Nobody here at all but him.

Where was everyone?

Was he the last person still left in Massapequa?

Or—the horrible thought started to batter at his frightened mind—was he the last person *anywhere*? Had something terrible happened, stranding him here, all alone?

What was going on? Was there anyone else? Anyone else left at all?

CHAPTER 2

SKYE BARNETT TRIED to cope by being grim and determined. It was all she had left to keep her fraying emotions in check. If she didn't have a purpose to focus on, she knew she'd scream, go all hysterical, and collapse in tears. And that was something she'd *never* do. She'd made herself that promise as a child, and she wasn't going to break it now, just because it was the end of the world or something.

Waking up all alone had been one of her worst nightmares since she was a baby. She'd never known her father. Mom had simply told Skye that he'd decided that the responsibilities of family life were too much for him, and he was giving up on it. "It," in this case, being Mom and the baby Skye. He'd not come to this decision all alone, apparently, but had been helped by his secretary, who'd abandoned her own life, too. The pair of them had skipped New York and headed west somewhere. Mom had never been able to find him to try and get child support or anything. Not that Mom had tried too hard.

Mom was all Skye had had since she was a child. Mom's parents were both dead, and Dad's parents were apparently uninterested in their granddaughter. Bitterly, Mom had insisted that they didn't need charity from anyone. The noble martyr, Skye would think unkindly. The truth was, Skye would have found her mother's excuse more believable if she hadn't made such a charity case of herself. Mom was lucky in one sense, because she was a Wall Street broker, and that paid pretty well, even given the rents in the city. And she was good at her work. She knew which stock would rise, and which would fall. The problem was that Mom had disastrous instincts when it came to boyfriends. None of them ever lasted very long. They were all bad bets. Losers. And it seemed like Mom—*and* Skye—always ended up paying the price.

It hadn't helped matters that Mom was not technically divorced. She'd never bothered to file—that chased off the few guys that got serious. After all, what was the point hanging around? And none ever did.

More typical were the ambitious, young hot shots, the kind of men who looked down on Skye as some sort of a parasite sucking blood from his girlfriend. Or else an anchor chaining her mom down. Occasionally Skye reluctantly would be included in ski weekends, but mostly she ended up being baby-sat by Mrs. Lopez across the hall. She spent those nights wondering if her mother would ever bother coming back for her, or if she'd just run off like Dad had.

But Mom had always come back.

Until this morning.

Skye tried to clamp down on her feelings, but it was so very difficult. Her insides felt as if someone had hacked at them with a dull knife. It hurt clean through her body.

Mom had gone out on a date last night with somebody, and she'd come home late—and not alone, either. Skye had been waiting, restlessly awake, until hours past midnight when she heard her mother fumbling with the key at the door. Even at fifteen—too old for Mrs. Lopez to baby-sit anymore—she would experience suffocating anxiety attacks when left alone. Her relief was shortlived. From the muttered conversation Skye realized that Mom had brought a boyfriend back with her. "Great," she sighed. Another L she could carve on her bedpost. For Loser. She tried to get to sleep.

Skye hadn't ever had a boyfriend. Not because she wasn't pretty; she was. Everybody said that, and they meant it. It was because she scared off the guys. Most boys she had been with were just hoping to make out in their new cars or whatever. She would always ask: "Will you stay with me forever?" *That* scared off the guys! None of them wanted any sort of a commitment. Skye *needed* that commitment more than she needed a boyfriend.

Val Kinsky had even laughed at her. They had taken a

walk one evening and Val had steered them both down a deserted path to the park near her house. Skye knew what was coming. He tightend his arm around her shoulder.

When she asked him, he had actually recoiled, as if bitten.

"*Stay* with you? Not for five minutes, girl," he'd replied. "I've got things to do. Things to be. I don't need no girl holding me back."

"I won't hold you back," she had promised him. "I won't hold you at all. Val, I *need* you."

"Skye," Val had answered, "you're sick. Psycho. Touched in the head. This isn't for forever. It's just for now." He tried to kiss her. She turned away her face.

His eyes turned hard and mean. "Fine." He roughly pushed her away. "Forget it. You aren't worth wasting time over. Anyway, hanging out with you would probably make me crazy, too."

Was she crazy? Skye didn't know. Was it crazy to want to have someone stay with you? To want people you supposedly cared about to be there when they were supposed to be? If that was crazy, then she supposed she was certifiable.

Now she was alone. *Really* alone. When she had woken up, Mom and the new boyfriend were gone. Not a word, not an explanation. Not a note, not even breakfast ready for her. They were just gone. As Skye had always feared, even her mother had deserted her.

She was all alone in the world.

At first all she'd been able to do was to cry. She didn't

know how long she'd wept, but she'd cried out most of her fear, and some of her loneliness. All the soft part of her terror was gone. All that was left was a hard, rocky core, deep inside her. It felt as if it were a rock thrown up from a volcano, red-hot and burning at her insides. But she wouldn't let it consume her.

She'd tried fixing herself breakfast, but for some reason the power wasn't working. Maybe Mom hadn't paid the bill, and they'd been cut off. But that wasn't like Mom. She always paid bills on time. Then Skye had discovered that the water wasn't working, either. She'd gone across the hallway to Mrs. Lopez and knocked on the door. But there was no reply. She, too, must have gone out early.

Then Skye had walked to the small window in the living room and looked down onto Nineteenth Street.

She had always loved living in this area of New York, close to Union Square. There was always a bustle of people, and even she never felt alone there. People on their way to work, or to meet loved ones, or to school, or just tourists wandering along, enjoying the sights of the city. It was never empty.

Only today it was. The street was totally deserted.

Skye wasn't sure what time it was, but she figured it had to be at least 10:00 A.M. That meant that there really should be people out there, running about like rabbits. And cars, and most especially, the flood of yellow taxis that crammed the streets and honked their horns constantly.

Only the streets were empty, and she couldn't even hear a car engine, let alone the songs of the horns.

It didn't make any sense, and that scared Skye almost as much as her mother being missing. New York was the city that never slept. That's what they said in all the commercials. And now it not only slept, it hibernated.

Where was everybody?

She went down the stairs—the elevators weren't working, for some reason—and out onto Nineteenth Street, heading east for Broadway. This was one of the busiest places in the city, normally. Wall-to-wall people, vendors, cars, and cabs. Only today it was just her.

Nobody else.

Nervously she walked to the corner and peered down Broadway toward Union Square. The buildings were there, and the trees, but nothing else. There were no cars, no people, *nothing* alive in sight. No brazen pigeons, pushing for whatever food fell to the ground. No dogs, wanting to be walked and scooped up after. Nothing.

It was as if New York had become a ghost town overnight. Only even the ghosts were gone. There was just her and the city.

She walked along, staring at the shuttered shops and closed buildings. There were cars parked in the roads, but nobody in them. Just up ahead was a twenty-four-hour diner. Excitedly she ran toward it. But the diner was deserted. A couple of cups of coffee sat on the counter, along with a folded newspaper.

"Hello?" she called out. "Hello!" she checked the paper. It was the early morning edition! Someone *must* have been here! She called out again. And again.

It was as if whoever had been drinking the coffee had just got up and left it behind when they went. A few dollar bills peeked out at her from under a cup. What kind of waitress would leave without picking up her tip? she wondered.

She walked behind the counter into the kitchen. "Hello?" On the deli table she found a sandwich, half-prepared and just abandoned. Pastrami on rye, with pickle and tomato . . . She hated pastrami. The sight of the food reminded her that she was hungry. Skye hesitated for a moment, then shrugged. There was nobody here to pay anyway, and the food would only go to waste. She fixed herself a roast beef sandwich—she had to hack the meat with a knife, because there was no power for the slicing machines. It looked as though power was off all over the city. Then she left the deli, munching as she walked.

Where had everybody gone?

She was abruptly reminded of Mrs. Lopez's big family Bible. Mrs. Lopez was a devout Catholic, and when she baby-sat Skye she always read her a story from the Bible at night. Skye wasn't a firm believer in anything, but she had been comforted by much of what the Bible had to say. She liked the bit where God said: "I will never leave thee nor forsake thee." That was a promise she had longed to hear. Those warm feelings had lasted until Good Friday, when Mrs. Lopez had read to her the passage about Jesus being crucified and crying out: "My God, My God, why hast thou forsaken me?"

That had terrified her so much she'd actually cried. Mrs.

Lopez had thought it was because she was afraid for Jesus, but that hadn't really been it. If God would forsake even his own Son, then why would he ever bother to look after someone as insignificant as Skye Barnett?

She'd felt even more lonely and abandoned after that.

But what she was now remembering was the story of what would happen when Jesus came back to Earth. Mrs. Lopez had read to her from the book of Revelations, most of which she didn't understand (and suspected that Mrs. Lopez didn't, either). And she'd explained to Skye that Jesus would take the saints up to Heaven first, before the end of the world, in something called the Rapture.

Was that what had happened here? Had Jesus come again, and taken all the people to Heaven with him, and left only her here on Earth, because she didn't believe in him strongly enough? Was she being punished for her wickedness by being abandoned forever?

To Skye, this was her idea of hell. To be left, alone, forever . . . What could be worse? She had this image of God being furious with her for her lack of faith, and condemning her to spend eternity alone.

No!

This had to just be her fear talking. The Rapture couldn't have happened, because the Bible stressed that some would be taken and at least as many left. This wasn't that at all. Here *everyone* but her seemed to have vanished.

On the other hand, New York is a big city. There might be other people about, perhaps even people who knew what was happening. It was just a matter of finding them. But how could she do that? She could search for days like that, and she didn't like the idea of spending even one night on her own. She was keeping her fear in check for now, but it was still lurking there, just below her surface calm. It would take only the tiniest spark to ignite an explosion that'd take possession of her body the first chance it got. She knew that. So she had to *act,* to do something so that the fear couldn't take control of her.

She had to think logically. She'd finished the sandwich, and she stopped at another all-night deli. Like everywhere else, it was deserted. But, it *was* well stocked. She grabbed an iced tea. Well, it was a lukewarm tea now, since the power was off, but it was better than nothing. Sitting at one of the tables, she wondered what she should do.

Okay, work it out logically. If there were other people still left in New York, where might they be? Well, any- where; that was the problem. She'd been abandoned on Nineteenth Street, so anyone else might have woken up anywhere. She had to assume that there were other people. She couldn't bear the thought of being the only person in the city. It was a huge place, and depressing in its silence. Silence . . .

That was the answer! It was so silent that if she made noise, it would be heard all over the city, probably. What sort of noise, though?

She glanced out of the deli window, and grinned to her- self. Across the street was a large electronics shop, the kind that peddles overpriced cellular phones to rich but clueless yuppies. And stereos. And *boom boxes* . . . Okay, the electricity was out, but most of those things ran off batteries, and they should be fine.

Finishing the iced tea, she threw the bottle into the recyclables can, and then laughed at herself. Who did she think was going to come and recycle the bottles right now? It was just habit, she knew. Skye crossed the street and looked in the store window. The door was shuttered closed, but that wasn't too much of a problem, really. She looked around, almost guiltily, as if expecting a policeman to show up. *Yes, please!* She was still alone, of course. Picking up a garbage can from the curb, she swung it and threw it at the window with all of her strength.

The shattering of the glass sounded incredibly loud in the silent world. Slivers cascaded down across everything. For a second Skye expected to hear a burglar alarm howl, but of course, it didn't. No power.

She brushed aside the glass and clambered gingerly through the broken window. She kicked aside the stuff she didn't need and jumped down into the main shop. There were shelves and shelves of radios, phones, calculators, date books, cameras, and computers. She walked to where the boom boxes were, and selected the biggest, meanest-looking one she could find. Checking the back showed it took batteries, so she raided the clipboard racks for the requisite number. She looked around and found a stack of CDs. It really didn't matter which ones she played, of course, but since she aimed to blast it, she figured it had better be something she could at least stomach hearing. *Enya*? Yeah, right. She found a Beastie Boys disc. That's better, she thought. A country CD caught her eye. She smiled. Slotting it in, she turned on the power.

A small red light lit up.

She laughed, happily. She'd been right! Batteries still worked! She hit *play,* and then turned up the volume control.

Tammy Wynette slammed out "Stand By Your Man," annihilating the silence. *Don't I wish I could,* Skye thought, but she refused to give in to despair. Instead, she hauled the boom box up, pocketed the other CD, and headed back out into the street through the broken window. As she walked, music blared out, echoing down the deserted streets.

Someone is bound to hear this, Skye worked at convincing herself. *I can't be the only person left in New York. I can't be . . .*

She could only pray that she was telling herself the truth.

CHAPTER 3

NICK STOOD IN the middle of the street, lost in despair. There was nobody. No matter which way he turned. Every where he was became the center of his own private, silent hell. Silence. It was like a powerful force now, with him right in the center of it. And he was getting more and more scared.

Everyone . . . gone. Everywhere?

Or just Massapequa? Nassau County? The whole of Long Island? New York? The United States?

The world?

Nick thought, am I losing my mind? He screamed: "Am I losing my mind?"

This was only terrifying him. He couldn't be the last man on earth. That was insane . . .

He remembered an episode of a television show he'd seen once about this mild-mannered guy who'd only wanted some peace and quiet to read a book. A bomb goes off and he ends up as the last man on Earth. So, cool, now he has loads of time to read. A dream come true. Only he breaks his glasses. Was something like that happening to him?

Thank goodness he didn't need glasses!

Nick remembered all of the times he'd wished he could be left alone to do whatever he wanted. Like when Briony was being extra bratty. She delighted in picking on him and irritating him. So many times he'd wished that she'd just vanish. And now she had. It made him feel kind of guilty.

Or when Mom had picked on him for not doing his homework, or being generally untidy, or raiding the fridge between meals. He'd wanted her just to leave him alone. And now he was alone—very alone. Or when Dad nagged him to try out for all the teams going, because he'd been a minor football star in his day. Nick didn't care much for sports, and that had really bugged Dad. He was forever trying to get Nick enthusiastic for some team or other, and Nick had just wanted Dad to drop it and leave him alone.

Talk about getting your wish—in spades!

He'd always wanted to be alone, but only at certain times. Not *all* the time.

Nick didn't have a clue as to what had happened to everyone, but he simply couldn't believe that he was the last person on Earth. There had to be other people somewhere; survivors who had escaped whatever had gone on here. All he had to do was to find them.

Easier said than done. How would he find anybody? Was there anyone else left in Massapequa at all? Even if there was, it was a sprawling town, and there was no way of knowing where anybody else might be. He couldn't just walk around, hoping to bump into somebody.

What he needed was a plan. And he wasn't really all that good at planning. But he had to figure this out logically. And for that, he needed food. He always thought better when he was eating. He went back into the house and checked the fridge. There were some cold cuts, a slice of congealed pizza, and some burgers. Burgers would be good, but the gas was out, and he couldn't cook them.

The barbecue grill! That ran on propane, and that should still be good!

He headed into the garden with a book of matches, hoping he was right. A burger just now was exactly what he needed for brain food. He turned on the tap at the propane tank, and then struck a match. He turned the switch on the control panel and held the match close to the grill. There was a hissing sound, and then the grill sprang to life.

Hallelujah! It worked!

The burger meat wasn't exactly cold, but it could hardly have spoiled this fast, he hoped. He grilled himself a couple of burgers, toasted the buns, and then added a ton of ketchup. Top it off with a glass of slightly cool Coke and he had a meal. As he munched, he concentrated on his problem.

He didn't have any idea if anyone else was still around or not. Walking around and looking was hardly likely to be any use. Aside from the fact it would tire him out really fast, it would mean he'd have to depend on pure chance if he came across anybody. If there *was* anybody.

So try again. If there *were* other people around, where would they be? Well, anywhere, of course. But would they *stay* anywhere? No. Logically, they'd be looking for other people, too. And where would they look?

They'd go somewhere major, of course. Somewhere there might be answers. Definitely not Massapequa. Maybe town hall? But he didn't have much of a clue as to where that might be, either.

There was only one place he could think of, and it made perfect sense to him. If there was anybody at all left in the entire area, they'd head for New York City. Which meant that he'd have to go there, too.

He doubted that the trains were still running, and he surely wasn't going to try walking all that way. Which left the car . . .

Technically, he was too young to drive it. He'd only just been given his learner's permit on his birthday, but he'd taken a few lessons in the Taurus. He was pretty sure he could drive it without any problem. Okay, he'd most likely stall out, and it might take a while to get the hang of things, but—well, he wasn't likely to crash into another car, let's face it. And there weren't exactly a lot of pedestrians he might run down.

The Taurus it was, then. He could drive into New York and look for others. If it was only Massapequa that was deserted, for some reason, then he'd run into other people on the way. Any way he thought about it, he was sure he was making the right decision. Of course, if Dad came home and found the car gone, he'd go ballistic. But Nick would take that chance. It would be worth getting yelled at and grounded for the rest of his life, just as long as he got his family back.

He turned off the grill but didn't bother cleaning up the dishes. There really wasn't any point to it. He grabbed his jacket, and the car keys from the box by the front door. What else should he take with him? Food? Drink? No, no point. If the world was deserted, he could take what he needed. If it wasn't, he'd find someone to help out. Money? He snorted. Was there really any point in that? What was there to buy when there was nobody to pay?

In the end, he just left everything. He didn't bother locking the house. After all, who was likely to try and rob it? He opened the garage doors and climbed into the Taurus. Okay, check the routine . . . Key in, ignition on. The sound of the engine was really loud. He'd forgotten how quiet things had become. Then ease into drive and release the break. Down on the accelerator.

The car jerked forward and stalled.

Cripes! He had to do better than that! He was glad that there wasn't anybody around to see him screw up like this. Okay, try again.

The second time, he got the car in motion, moving gently forward and into the road. He accelerated slightly, going up to twenty miles per hour as he approached the corner, and signaled a turn. Then he laughed. Who did he think he was warning with that indicator? It was just habit, of course.

He headed for Sunrise Highway, going slowly and looking around as he went. He didn't want to miss seeing anyone else who might be around. Then, again, he winced at his own stupidity. Anyone who was around was bound to hear the car—it was making the only noise in town! They would have to come and investigate.

It was really weird, driving through the neighborhood and not seeing kids playing, people talking, dogs wandering around, or anything at all moving. No birds darting from tree to tree, no squirrels scurrying for food. Nothing at all but the silent, empty houses and gardens and roads.

Nick shivered, and inched up the speed a little. He was getting the hang of this.

Sunrise Highway was deserted. There were a couple of parked cars by the shops, and for a second he felt hope. Maybe somebody had just gone looking for food or something. But he realized they were simply cars that had been parked when people had vanished. It was eerie, like driving through a cemetery, where no one was alive but you didn't actually see any bodies.

That thought made him uncomfortable. Was it possible that somehow everyone but him was dead? But it didn't make sense. What on earth could kill everyone, and yet spare him? It simply didn't make sense.

Was *he* dead? That sudden thought almost made him swerve off the road. His head pounded as he corrected for the mistake. No, that couldn't be the answer. For one thing, he didn't *feel* dead. He felt absolutely normal. For another, if he were dead, why would he be here, in a deserted world? He'd never heard of any kind of an afterlife like that.

It was no good trying to think of answers to the mystery, he realized, because he simply didn't have any facts to go on. Aside from the fact that everyone seemed to have vanished. And all of the animals, too. He couldn't think of a single force that could make both humans and animals evacuate the area. And definitely none that would make his family simply abandon him. He'd just have to shelve the problem for now, and hope to come across further information sometime to help out. Right now his main concern was finding other . . . what? survivors? That implied everyone was dead, and he wasn't about to do that. Abandoned? But that implied he'd been deliberately left behind, and that didn't make any sense, either. People. That was it! Other people . . .

He'd been driving for about fifteen minutes and saw no signs of anything moving, save for a flag in the wind and a few tree branches. No people, no animals, no life. Just himself, driving along an empty, lonely road. He turned off to head toward the Long Island Expressway. That was the easiest route to New York, and the one any other *people* would take, too. If there was anyone else around, that was his best bet of finding them.

He was driving through a different area now, one he didn't really know too well. Houses and shops lined the streets, all silent and still. A few cars and trucks were parked off the edge of the road. There were no signs of their owners, or of what might have happened. Feeling increasingly lonely and scared, he made it to the expressway.

"The world's longest parking lot," the joke went. He remembered any number of days with his family, trying to drive into the city and getting stuck in traffic. Accidents, rubbernecking, and just plain, lousy crowds kept the expressway from being anything like express. Traffic construction, bad driving, and sheer volume clogged the roads. But today . . .

Nothing. Bare stretches of empty concrete, stretching away in front of him. Not a car in sight, save for one abandoned beside the road from time to time, with police stickers warning the owners to move them. He saw a police car parked off the side once, and slowed, hoping against hope. But it must have been a traffic cop, waiting in hiding for prey that never came. Now it, too, was empty.

Nick drove on, amazed to see that he was doing fifty now. He was getting more used to this driving thing. Of course, it helped having no other traffic to cope with! He'd give anything to run into a snarl of cars, angry motorists, and honking horns.

It was smooth driving all of the way.

Finally he crested the bridge beside Calvary Cemetery, and New York was spread out in front of him. He avoided looking at the cemetery, not wanting to connect it with the world at large. He slowed the car to a stop and stared out at the famous skyline of Manhattan. The Empire State Building, the Chrysler Building, the Twin Towers . . . all spread out beautifully in front of him. It made him ache, looking at it.

And there hadn't been a sign of anyone else at all the entire drive in. A beautiful sight, New York in the morning—but was he the only person left to see it?

Nick turned off the engine and climbed out of the car. He stood there, in the middle of the road, listening and looking. Nothing. Nobody. No sounds, nothing moving. There was a lump in his throat. Was he, somehow, then, the last person on earth? He simply couldn't think of anything that might have emptied out this great city without a problem, overnight. He couldn't see any movement on the roads, no helicopters buzzing about, no planes overhead. There were no lights on. It was dead.

Could he have been wrong? Maybe there wasn't anyone else at all.

No! He refused to believe that. Whatever had happened, he couldn't be alone. Much as he liked peace and quiet, there were limits that a person could take!

He jumped back into the car again and started it up. He was definitely getting the hang of this, but what was the point? If he was alone, he could drive anywhere, do anything he wanted. And none of it would make any difference or any sense.

Then he saw the car radio. Maybe someone was around, and they were broadcasting messages! He hadn't even thought to try picking up a radio station. Dumb! He turned on the radio and set it to scan automatically as he drove.

It cycled through the whole band width without stopping. Scared and irritated, he tuned it to FM and tried again. Still silence. With a sinking heart, he turned off the radio. Scratch another idea.

It was getting harder and harder to believe that anyone was left. If there were any officials at all around, they were bound to get some sort of message out. So it looked like there weren't any. Maybe this idea of going to New York was really dumb, after all, and he might as well have stayed at home. But the idea that he was all that was left was simply too terrible to believe in. He *had* to have other people around. He couldn't be all there was . . .

Nick reached the toll booths at the Midtown Tunnel and slowed. They obviously wouldn't be working, with no power. But at the far right was a lane reserved for official traffic. Well, he was as official as anyone today, so he drove past the empty booths and through it. Then he headed into the tunnel itself.

It was absolutely dark in there, just a few feet from the entrance. Of course—no power, no lights. He turned on the car's headlights—after turning off the wipers he accidentally started first—and that enabled him to see his way ahead. As he crawled uncertainly along the length of the tunnel, he suddenly realized there was a light on the dashboard blinking at him. *Fuel* . . . Oh, great—he was on empty and hadn't even realized it. Dad hadn't gassed up the car . . . He prayed that it wouldn't give out, and it almost worked. The engine died just short of the far exit.

Oh, well. It had done its job, getting him here. He could see daylight ahead at the end of the tunnel, so it wouldn't be too rough a walk. He removed the keys and then looked at them. The car key, the house key, and a couple of others he couldn't identify. What did he need with them now? They were no good to him at all. Dropping the keys onto the passenger seat, he climbed out of the car, slamming the door shut automatically.

He felt like he was abandoning everything he had ever known, walking away from the family car and toward the city ahead of him. It was almost symbolic, in kind of a crazy way. As if he was leaving the past behind and entering . . . what?

He walked out of the tunnel, past repair work, and out onto the street. As he'd been dreading, it was still empty. Nobody at all was around.

Where should he go? Nick considered the idea. New York was an island, but it was still a very large place. If there was anybody around, where would they be? Somewhere really obvious, they'd have to be . . .

The Empire State Building! The most famous building in New York, if not the world. If there was anybody around, surely that was where they would be. He couldn't remember its exact address, except it was on Fifth Avenue, but how hard could it be to find the tall building? He wandered across to Thirty-fifth Street, and saw the spike of the building not too far away.

Okay! He'd just head for that, and if there was anyone else . . .

He stopped dead, holding his breath, afraid that he was imagining things. His heart was pounding loudly in his ears, but even over that, he was certain that he could make out the strains of music.

It sounded like a faint country and western song . . .

There *was* somebody else! He wasn't alone! There were other people!

He began running toward the beautiful, beautiful sound.

CHAPTER 4

SKYE WASN'T WALKING with anywhere particular in mind. She'd started out simply walking north, because it was a direction. The boom box was loud and quite heavy, but she had no intention of abandoning it for a lighter one. Even if it didn't attract other people, at least it made her feel a bit better, hearing some noise. It was hard to realize how adjusted you could get to the sounds of the city.

She crossed Madison Square and hit Fifth Avenue. Shrugging, she started up it. It was as good a direction as any. She didn't have any aim, and she was trying to avoid thinking about all the problems she had. But she couldn't help wondering what would happen when night fell. Normally she loved New York at night. The lights, the sounds, the people—they all made it rather magical.

But none of them would be here when darkness fell. New York would be blacked out, silent and empty, apart from her. Skye was having enough trouble holding herself together during the day. How would she ever be able to cope if she had to spend a dark, silent night alone?

She wiped tears from her cheeks, hardly realizing she'd been crying. She felt like a small child again, when her father had abandoned her. Now *everyone* had abandoned her, and she was alone in this vast, deserted concrete jungle. She set down the boom box and hugged herself, crying and letting her emotions spill out.

Alone . . .

She'd never be able to take it. Skye knew this. She'd go mad, or kill herself, or something. She would never survive being on her own. Maybe God *was* punishing her, after all. She wasn't even sure she believed in him, but she felt like she was being singled out for punishment.

But that was really crazy. Surely, if anyone had been punished by a vengeful God, it was all of those who'd vanished. She'd been left behind, for whatever reason. "Why?" she whispered to a God she didn't know. "Why have you done this to me?"

There was no answer. Maybe, if there was a God, he'd left New York City as well.

After a while, she wiped her face, picked up the boom box, and kept on walking. She could hardly get any more depressed, but standing there crying wasn't helping any. At least while she walked, she felt like she was doing *something*. Whether there was any point to it, of course, she couldn't tell.

It was past noon now, and she was starting to wonder about eating again. That made her wonder about food. The fresh stuff would start going off really fast. It was only spring, so it wasn't too hot yet, but the food was bound to spoil. Unless, of course, all the bacteria had vanished with the people and animals and birds. In which case it would simply dry up. Either way, it would be inedible in a day or so. After that, of course, there was canned food, and packaged food, and so on. There had to be more than enough of that in the city to last her a lifetime, however long she lived. Of course, without electricity or gas, she'd have to eat it cold. Or maybe start campfires . . .

She had to giggle at the thought of having a cookout in a city park somewhere. Toasting marshmallows in Central Park, maybe . . .

Skye caught herself, realizing she was on the verge of hysterics. She couldn't let herself go like that! She'd only been on her own a few hours at most, and she was already starting to crack. What would happen after days or weeks of this sort of life? Assuming, as a sort of worst-case scenario, that she was alone. Horrible thought.

No! She had to get a grip on herself. She rested again, her hand all red from carrying the heavy boom box. She was up to Thirtieth Street, and saw the Empire State Building looming ahead. She grinned again when she realized she'd been walking on the sidewalk, purely out of instinct.

As if it might be dangerous right now walking down the middle of the deserted street!

The disc finished, so she switched it for the other she'd brought. The brief silence had unnerved her, and she was glad to have the noise back again. LeAnn Rimes belted forth, and Skye started out again.

And then frowned.

She could have sworn she'd heard something, even over the noise of the song. Or was it just wishful thinking? Was she going really crazy already? Quickly she hit the *pause* button on the machine.

"Hey! Hold on!"

Skye spun around, almost dropping the boom box as she did so. There, coming down the side street at a run, waving his arms, was a boy! She set the player down, staring at him almost in disbelief, and then ran across to meet him.

A few paces away, the boy stopped, rather self-consciously, but she didn't care. Skye grabbed him and hugged him tight. "You're real!" she exclaimed happily. "You are! I'm not all alone!"

"I was going to say something like that," the boy gasped. "But it would be easier if you didn't hug me quite so hard."

"Oh." Skye let him go but didn't back off. She was half-afraid that if she left him, he'd vanish like everybody else. "I'm sorry."

"It's okay," he answered, grinning. "Like I said, I feel pretty much the same way you do. I guess you've not met anyone else, then?"

"No," Skye confessed. "Only you. I thought everyone was gone, and I was all alone. You don't know how glad I am to find you."

"I think I do," he replied. "About as glad as I am to have found *you*. I drove in from Massapequa, and you're the only person I've seen all day."

Skye had to think about that for a second. "From Long Island? There's nobody there, either?"

"There doesn't seem to be anyone anywhere," he answered. "But, of course, there's a lot of ground neither of us has covered." He looked hard at her again. "I am just so glad to have found somebody else. I was getting kind of lonely."

"Me too," Skye admitted. "I don't think I could take being alone in the city at night. It's going to get very dark and very quiet."

The boy sobered. "Yeah, I guess it is. I hadn't thought that far ahead." He gestured at the boom box. "That was a really great idea. I heard the music all the way from the Midtown Tunnel. You don't know how terrific it made me feel." He suddenly held out his hand. "I'm Nick Morganthau, by the way."

"Skye Barnett," she answered, shaking his hand. It felt so horribly insufficient, even if terribly civilized. Shaking his hand, when he might just have saved her sanity. She grabbed him and hugged him again, not quite as tightly this time. "You don't know how terrific this makes me feel."

"Trust me," Nick answered, his face buried in her hair. "Being hugged by a pretty girl isn't exactly hard on me, either."

"Don't take that the wrong way," she warned him, letting go of him abruptly. "I don't usually go around hugging strangers."

"Unless they're the only person left with you in the city," he agreed. "I kind of guessed that. I'm not usually a hug recipient, except from my mom. Relax, I won't take advantage of you."

"Damned right you won't," she growled. But she couldn't stay mad for long. It felt too good having someone else around. "Do you think there'll be more people coming?"

"Tired of my company already?" he asked her, putting on a pretend scowl.

"No!" Skye felt a sudden surge of panic. He couldn't be mad enough to walk out on her, surely? "I didn't mean that! I was just wondering if there were any more, or if we were it."

Nick shrugged. "There's no way of knowing. All we can do is to wait and see if anyone else shows up. Where were you heading?"

"Nowhere in particular," she confessed. "I was just walking because . . ." She couldn't admit that it was so she wouldn't have to think. "Well, just walking."

He nodded. "Yeah. I thought that if anyone *did* come to New York, they'd head for the Empire State Building. It's the most obvious place. I was heading there myself."

Skye thought about that. "Good idea," she agreed. "It's a real landmark, and a good place to gather. Shall we go on together?"

"You kidding?" Nick asked. "Now I've found you, I'm sticking right next to you constantly. I don't want to be alone again."

"Me neither," Skye confessed. She felt so much better now she was no longer alone. The mad panic that had been hammering at her self-control was gone. She was still scared, because she didn't understand what was happening. But at least it could be endured, now that there was someone to share it with. Skye blushed, thinking: He isn't exactly bad-looking, either. And around my age. She felt so much better. True she'd have been happy even if he'd been a doddering eighty-year-old! Not to be alone anymore? *That* was what mattered.

They walked back to where she'd left the boom box, and he picked it up for her. She hit the *play* key, and LeAnn started singing once again. She turned it down slightly, so they could talk while they walked the last few blocks.

"Skye's a nice name," Nick commented. "Is it short for Schuyler? Or one of those River Phoenix types of names?"

"Neither," she answered. "It's an island off the coast of Scotland. My family is very big on roots." She laughed a kind of apologetic laugh.

"Oh." Nick nodded, his thoughts directed elsewhere. He was thinking of his own family. "My folks and my kid sister all vanished. I never thought I'd miss the brat, but I do." For a second Skye thought he might burst out crying. She wasn't sure what to do. But she knew exactly how he felt.

"I've just lost my mom," Skye said. "My father vanished years ago."

Nick gave her a confused look. ''Sorry to hear that,'' Nick commented. ''It's got to be hard, being an only kid, I suppose. And with no dad.''

''It was . . . rough,'' she replied, understating the case. ''I was getting really scared, being on my own.''

''To be honest, so was I.'' He stopped. ''Well, here we are.'' He set down the player and peered through the doors. No sign of a security guard anywhere. He pushed on the revolving door. It was locked. That made sense—it would be locked overnight.

''I think you'll have to break it,'' Skye suggested. He looked at her uncertainly. ''I know it seems wrong, but . . .'' She shrugged.

Nick nodded. ''Hey, I'll be happy to spend the night in jail if I'm arrested. I'd just be so happy to see a cop.'' He used one of the trash cans to shatter the glass. It wasn't nearly as easy as he would have thought. ''Not at all like in the movies,'' he grunted.

Skye laughed. ''It never is.''

He carefully knocked out the sharp slivers that jutted from the frame before stepping through. Glass crunched under his feet. ''Maybe you should leave the music outside,'' he suggested. ''People will hear it better.''

''*If* there's anyone else,'' Skye agreed, setting down the player. Then she followed him into the deserted foyer.

She'd been inside the Empire State building a dozen times in her life, but never when it was so empty. It was spooky. They walked quietly past darkened shop windows to the information desk. Nick grinned at her.

"Boy, what I'd give for some information right now," he said. He pretended to be a tourist asking a question of a clerk. "Excuse me, miss, but you don't have any clue what happened to everyone, do you?"

"No," Skye confessed, preening innocently. "But here's an I Love New York bumper sticker. And enjoy your stay." They both laughed. Then Skye turned serious again. "I really don't know what happened. I keep thinking up possibilities, but they're all too crazy to be true."

"Me too," Nick admitted. He felt a fluttering panic returning, and smothered it with an act of will. "I guess we'll just have to hope that somebody does turn up who knows what happened here." He glanced around. "You know," he said, changing the subject, "this is the first time I've ever been in here. It's kind of nice. But I think I'll skip the rooftop view. I wouldn't want to have to climb over a hundred floors!"

"Me neither," Skye agreed, laughing. "I've been up a lot of times, though. I grew up in the city."

That made him brighten. "Hey, that's great. So you know where everything is, then?"

Skye laughed, and turned her hands palm up like a stop sign. "Hardly everything. But probably enough things. What were you after?"

"Well, we'd better start doing some planning ahead," he suggested. "First of all, we're going to need somewhere to stay. I mean, this place is great, but I don't think it has anywhere to sleep. How about your home?"

Skye shook her head. "I don't think I want to go back

there without my mom,'' she said softly. ''It would be too hard. Besides . . . we've got the whole city to choose from. Why go back to a dinky apartment when we've got the world's most luxurious accommodations all around us?''

''I like your thinking,'' Nick said, grinning. ''As long as we've here, why not go for the best? Uh . . . what *is* the best?''

''The Plaza,'' she said without hesitation. ''It's up by Central Park, and it's the most spectacular hotel in the city.''

Nick grinned. ''Expensive?''

She purred, ''Obscenely expensive.''

''Alright! let's go.''

''Let's check in there later,'' suggested Skye. ''I think we should hang around here for the time being, in case anyone else comes.'' She paused. ''Though I think a change in music is in order. I'm getting sick of hearing LeAnn Rimes over and over again.''

''So am I,'' Nick agreed.

''There's a record store a block north,'' said Skye.

''Cool. Let's check it out after lunch.'' He glanced around the lobby. ''There's got to be two things around here somewhere.''

''What?'' she asked.

''First, somewhere to eat. Second, a janitor's closet.''

Skye frowned. ''Okay, you've got me. I can see why you want the first, but why the second?''

He laughed. ''I want something to help us break into places that's easier to wield than a garbage can. A crowbar would be perfect, but I'll settle for a good, solid broom handle. I think we're going to be doing a lot of breaking and entering.''

"Quite the career criminals," Skye giggled.

"Yeah. Well, I wouldn't mind being arrested. Just as long as I'm not put into solitary."

The thought made her shudder. She grabbed his hand. "I don't think I could stand that," she admitted. "Nick, the idea of being all alone terrifies me. Promise you won't leave me. *Promise*!''

Nick swallowed hard. "Skye," he began, "I wish I could—"

"You have to!" She was on the verge of hysteria. Nick felt himself pulling away. Maybe it *was* true that native New Yorkers were all mental cases. "Please, Nick," she insisted. "You don't understand. I couldn't bear to lose you now. Not ever!''

"Skye," he said gently. "Listen to me. It might not be my decision."

She blinked at him, not certain what he meant.

"Trust me, if it was up to me, I'd promise. But we still don't know why everyone else vanished overnight." He paused. "We have to consider the possibility that one or both of us might also vanish tonight. Until we know what happened, there aren't any guarantees for either of us."

Skye seemed to slump. It was a horrible thought, she realized, but Nick was right. There *were* no guarantees. But she'd do whatever she could to stay safe. She gripped his hand tightly. "Then I'm not letting you out of my sight," she vowed.

Nick squeezed back, to reassure her. Or maybe to reassure himself. Then he smiled at her. "We'll deal with those problems when they arise, I guess. Right now I vote for food, before it all goes off. Where can a guy get a bite to eat around here?"

Skye let go of his hand, then composed herself. After a while, she told him about a small café down the block. "This way," she said. She felt her confidence returning. "And then we'll look for your janitor's closet. I'd like to have a crowbar of my own."

"His and hers," Nick joked.

Skye grinned. No guarantees. That's what Nick had said. She tried to look on the bright side. True, something very scary was going on. But she wasn't facing it alone. And there were a lot worse people she could have been stuck with than him.

Maybe there *were* others out there. Others just like them. And if not, well, at least she had Nick.

A thought blew through her mind like a chill breeze. Yes, I have Nick. *But for how long?*

She found herself shivering.

CHAPTER 5

As THEY ATE their sandwiches, Nick thought about Skye. On the one hand, she had practically saved his life. Not to be alone was so reassuring. Skye was really pretty—gorgeous brown eyes, a long, thick mane of dark hair, and a nice figure. How many times had he daydreamed about being shipwrecked on a deserted island with a supermodel? Well, this wasn't too bad. Yeah, he grinned to himself, it could be a *lot* worse. Plus, she wasn't all stuck up and full of herself. Nick found out that he really liked just talking with her.

Except . . .

She was crushingly needy. And she was terrified of being alone. Not like a scary movie sort of fear. This was a fear like a panic. She *needed* to be with him. All the time. So she'd been abandoned by her father, and her mother didn't have a lot of time for her. Lots of kids have that happen. This was more serious.

When he'd excused himself to go to the bathroom, she'd almost broken down. He'd half expected her to want to follow him and hold his hand, but she had at least realized that was overdoing it. But she had waited outside, breathing so hard she was hyperventilating, until he'd come out again. She'd had the same problem when it was her turn. She'd rushed as fast as she could.

"Skye," he said gently, as they picked through CDs in the local store, "you have to relax a bit."

"Relax?" she asked, her eyes haunted. "How *can* I relax? Nick, everybody in the world, maybe, but the two of us have vanished, and you want me to *relax*? Are you crazy?"

Nick wanted to reply: *No, but you are . . .* But he didn't. He knew it wouldn't go over too well. "I understand that," he said. "But we can't live on the edge of hysterics forever. You have to realize that there simply aren't any certainties right now. I promise I'll stay right with you if it's in my power to do so. But I won't give you a promise that I might not be able to keep."

She gathered her strength, and nodded. "I understand, Nick. I do. It's just that . . . you can't imagine how terrible it is to be all alone, and unwanted. I know I overdo it, but I can't help it. I panic."

"Yes, I kind of noticed that." He smiled gently at her. "So we'll have to work on it, that's all. How are you doing with the music?"

She held up half a dozen discs. "Pretty good. How about you?"

"The same. I guess they will keep us sane this afternoon. We could work our way through the whole store with time." He took a bag and filled it with spare batteries. "Wouldn't want the power to run out on us."

They headed back to the Empire State Building and spent the rest of the afternoon there. Most of the time they were either in the lobby or exploring, and simply allowed the music to play on till they had to change it. Together they found a crowbar in a closet, which made things simpler when they wanted to break into places. They also came across a gun in the drawer of one of the offices.

Skye looked at it. "Maybe we should take it," she suggested.

"What for?" Nick was puzzled. "There are no dangerous animals, and hardly any muggers left, even in New York."

She swallowed. "Not everybody is as nice as you," she said softly. "Some of Mom's boyfriends were . . . less than gentle."

Nick flinched. *I guess she really has been through the wars*, he thought. Abusive boyfriends, too. No wonder she was a bit skittish. "I'd rather not carry it," he admitted. "I don't like the thought of having to hurt anyone."

"They might not feel the same way," Skye pointed out.

"Maybe not," he agreed. "But we don't even know if there *are* any other people around. If it's all the same to you, I'd sooner not plan on shooting them."

After a moment, she nodded. "I guess you're right. But I'd feel a bit safer with a gun around."

"I wouldn't," he said firmly. "My cousin shot himself to death playing with one of those things. It's more dangerous to us than anyone we'd try to use it on."

"I'm sorry," Skye said quietly. She turned away, and he closed the drawer.

The afternoon went pretty well. They sat and talked mostly. The sun was getting low and the shadows had crept into the building now. "I think we'd better start out for the Plaza," he suggested. "We can come back here tomorrow morning and wait again."

"Sounds good," Skye agreed. She turned off the music and then grinned. "I guess we can leave this where it is. Nobody's likely to steal it."

"True enough." Nick followed her lead, heading up Fifth Avenue toward Central Park. "Maybe we'd better do some shopping on the way. Dinner would be nice."

"Yes," Skye admitted. "But I hate having sandwiches all the time."

"We don't have to," Nick answered. "All we need to do is find somewhere that sells camping supplies. Bottled gas works perfectly."

She looked surprised. "I never thought of that! In which case, I'm a pretty decent cook. I've had to fend for myself a lot. I'll make dinner."

That cheered him up. Burning toast and roasting burgers were about the limit of his cooking skills. "You're on," he agreed. "So we'd better find a food store, too. Bottled water could come in handy, for washing and stuff."

"And clean clothes," Skye added. "Let's face it, we

won't be able to do any laundry any time soon."

"We won't need to," Nick answered, hefting the crowbar. "Whatever takes your fancy, we can just take."

Skye grinned. "Better than an unlimited credit card."

Nick was pleased that she seemed so happy. Skye was moody, like night and day. But when she wasn't panicking, she was a fun companion. Together they went "shopping." The first thing Nick did was to get a small cart on which to load everything. Then they raided a sports store, finding a couple of good oil-fired burners. After that, Skye insisted on Bloomingdale's. They left the cart in the street and entered the darkening store. Nick had brought along a couple of heavy-duty flashlights, which were invaluable.

"You want to check out the women's wear?" he suggested. "I can go to men's, and then we can meet—"

"No!" Skye exclaimed, her eyes wide. "No, Nick. We have to stick together. If anything should happen to you, I don't know what I'd do."

Nick tried to be firm. "I'm not really into girl stuff. And it's only for a little while. You'll be okay."

She clutched wildly at his arm, like a drowning person clawing for a life preserver. She was shaking. "No. Come with me. *Please!* I promise not to take forever." She was really scared, he realized. How much of her fear was she managing to keep hidden from him? This thing she had about being alone must be affecting her very badly.

"Okay," he relented.

Skye led the way to the women's department, her good mood resurfacing. "So, what do you think this year's fashions are going to be?"

"Whatever you decide to wear," he answered. "You're going to be it in all the social circles."

She picked out a couple of tops, jeans, and a skirt. Nick found her a bag, and she placed her finds in it, adding a few pairs of underwear. "Your turn now," she said.

"You're not going to try them on?" Nick asked her. "I thought all girls had to try on a hundred things to buy one scarf."

"I'm not like other girls, then," Skye answered. "Besides, I'm not going into a changing room alone. And much as I like you, I'm not taking you in with me, either."

"Spoilsport," Nick answered, grinning to show he was only joking. It took him even less time than it had taken Skye to pick out a week's worth of socks, T-shirts, and underwear. Both of them found pajamas. Loading these onto the cart, they went in search of food. He let Skye pick whatever she wanted, adding potato chips, sodas, snacking cheese, and several bottles of water. Skye added toiletries, such as toothpaste and brushes.

With all of their hunting done, Skye led the way through the silent, shadowy streets to the Plaza. Nick was impressed with the opulence of the place. It was dark inside, but the flashlight beams picked out a lot of intricate details and the light glittered off the enormous chandeliers.

"Well, we can pick the best rooms in the place," Nick said. "Though I think the penthouse had better be out. I'd rather have something with less stairs to climb."

"First floor, definitely," Skye agreed. Then she winced. "Electronic locks," she muttered. "That could be a problem. We can't make up a key."

"But with the power down, the doors should be open," Nick pointed out.

"Are you sure?"

Nick grinned. "No. But I saw something similar on an episode of McGyver."

Skye rolled her eyes.

He grabbed a couple of the bags from the cart. "Let's go find us a place to sleep. Then you can play gourmet chef, and I can admire your skills."

Skye nodded, grabbing her clothes. "Okay."

They went to the first floor. Nick pushed at the first door they came to, and it did indeed swing open. "Told you," he crowed smugly. He shone the flashlight inside, and whistled. There were two large beds, very ornate, and a long, low dresser. There were ornate chairs at a table beside the window, and expensive looking prints on the wall. There were large closets and a separate bathroom. Enough light shone from the dying sun and their combined flashlights to show it was definitely a regal set of rooms.

"I could live with this," Nick said cheerfully. "So let's see if next door is good for you."

"Uh-uh," Skye said, looking scared again. "There's plenty of room for two here." She gazed at him with frightened eyes. "You *know* I can't be alone. I mean, I'm not suggesting anything between us, you know, but . . . I *can't* leave you tonight. If I woke up all alone in the night, I'd go crazy. I know I would."

Nick sighed inwardly. He'd half been expecting this. Skye was on the verge of cracking up, but she didn't seem to understand how uncomfortable this made him feel. Sharing a room with a very pretty, if flaky, girl was a bit more than he really wanted to do right now. After all, he'd barely known her a few hours ago. On the other hand, he didn't think she'd take no for an answer here. "I guess," he said reluctantly.

Letting her bags drop, Skye came over to him and took his hand. "Nick, I know this is hard for you. I mean, you probably think I'm just crazy, and that you'd be better off without me."

"No way," he said, forcing himself to sound more cheerful than he was. "Then I'd have to cook for myself, wouldn't I? And I'm a lousy cook."

She ignored his weak attempt at humor. "I know I'm obsessive about this, but I can't help it. I've been hurt so often in the past. I know I'm going to have trouble sleeping tonight. But it will help me immensely if I can see that you're still with me when I'm awake. I know I'd really go insane if I had to spend any length of time alone."

"I understand," he said, and he did, a little. She might be sixteen, but at night, in the dark, she was still a frightened child at heart. "It's okay. Now, how about dinner?"

Skye grinned happily, and they went downstairs. She fixed the food—pepper steak—and he had to admit that she was indeed a good cook. After the meal, they nibbled on potato chips and sipped warm soda and talked. She told him about some of her adventures in the city, and he told her of life out on the island. Nick found that he was really growing to like her.

Eventually, though, they were both exhausted. "We'd better get some rest," Nick decided. "Tomorrow could be a busy day. You know: places to go, people to meet." He grinned, to show he was joking. They went upstairs with the toiletries and water.

Skye picked up her pajamas. "I'll change in the bathroom," she said. "You can do it out here." Nick noticed that she left the door slightly ajar; she wasn't confident enough yet to close it completely. He changed as fast as he could, and slipped into his bed. A moment later, Skye came out. She padded across the luxuriously carpeted floor and put her flashlight down beside her bed. Then she sat on Nick's bed.

"Thank you," she said. "I . . . I truly do appreciate it." Then she leaned down and kissed his cheek. "Let's pray for sweet dreams."

"Definitely," he agreed, his cheek burning. He had never been kissed by a girl before. Not a real girl, anyway. Just his mom, and his grandmother. This was way different. The room was almost totally dark now, and he heard a silky rustling as she slipped in between her sheets. It was weird, he thought, sharing a room with a girl. He wasn't exactly sure what he was supposed to do next. He tried to breathe very quietly. At the same time, he had to confess that he, too, was scared that something might happen overnight; he might wake up to find Skye gone, too. Just like his folks.

It hurt him to think about his family. Where had his parents and Briony gone? It was a question with no answer that kept hammering on his brain. Over and over and over. Were they okay? Were they worrying about him, wherever they were? He felt choked, and had to calm himself down. All he had right now was Skye, and he was very glad he at least had her.

Think only about Skye, he told himself. He listened for her breathing, in and out, like gentle waves lapping on the shore. That's it, his brain told him. Think happy thoughts.

But reality came crashing down on him like a tidal wave. Always the same questions: *What happened to everyone?* Why had he and Skye been spared? By accident? Or by design? Did somebody intend for the two of them to meet? Were they the last people on Earth? Or were there others like them, scattered all across the globe?

Nick was certain that the disappearances had to be universal. If it had only been in New York, then there would have been planes from other countries flying overhead, looking to land at Kennedy Airport or something. Or there would be military aircraft investigating. The fact that they were still alone after a whole day tended to suggest that if there were others left on Earth, they were very few and scattered. Maybe there were small groups of people all over America—or the world—just getting together and hunting for others.

Perhaps other people would show up. It would be great if they did. But if they didn't?

What if he and Skye were it? The last boy and last girl on Earth?

Would they have to get married and work on repopulating the planet? That would be a long job!

But would they even have that chance? After all, since they didn't have any clue what had happened to everyone else on Earth, there was absolutely no guarantee that she or he wouldn't also vanish tonight . . .

There was a tight wad of pain in his stomach at this thought. He didn't want to lose Skye now!

It was hard getting to sleep. He tossed and turned like a rotisserie. Terrible thoughts flooded his mind. He could hear Skye turning restlessly in the other bed. It isn't any easier on her, he thought. If anything, it was probably a lot harder. She was probably trying to stay awake. It wouldn't work, though. They were both far too stressed out and tired to stay awake for very long.

Eventually Nick drifted off into a troubled, nightmare-plagued sleep . . .

CHAPTER 6

SKYE WOKE UP in a panic, her heart thundering in her chest, sweat dripping from her forehead. For a bewildered moment, she couldn't think why.

She was alone! Terrified, she opened her eyes. She could hardly breathe. She flung out her arms, clawing wildly at the darkness. "Nick!" she screamed.

Relief washed over her when she heard him turn over in his bed and sleepily mutter, "Huh?" He fell back to sleep, snoring. Skye let out her breath in a relieved grateful rush, she had only dreamed she was alone. Suddenly, her panic struck her as unreasonable and childish.

See . . . No reason to get all excited. She calmed herself.

A strange glow illuminated the room. She sat up, puzzled. It wasn't a full moon, and yet there was a wash of light in the room, pale but real.

They'd left the curtains open—after all, there was nobody to watch them!—and she saw that there was light outside. She clambered out of bed and padded to the window.

She could see the woods and fields of Central Park spread out below, and a mysterious light was shining *inside* it . . . It was moving slowly, as if something were carrying it.

People?

No . . . it couldn't be. There was no power, and the intensity of the light couldn't be generated by common batteries. Skye became frightened. She rushed to Nick's bed. "Nick!" she whispered urgently. She shook him awake.

He opened his eyes with a start, but Skye cupped her hand flat over his mouth. "Don't talk! Come and look at this!"

He swung his legs onto the floor, and took her hand away. "Look at what?" he asked, yawning. He blinked groggily. "Jeez, Skye, do you have any idea what time it is?"

"About three A.M.," she answered. "Come on!" She pulled at him until he levered himself off the bed and followed her sleepily to the window.

Then he woke up completely.

"What the heck?" he whispered.

"My thoughts exactly," said Skye. "There's something out there, Nick, and I don't like it. It must be whatever's behind the disappearances."

"Maybe not," he said. "Maybe it's people."

"What *kind* of people? And where would they get lights like that from?"

He shook his head and sighed. "We'd better get some clothes on. We have to check it out."

Skye froze. "You think that's safe?"

"No," Nick admitted. "But we've got to do it. This could be the answer to where everyone has gone. We can't just hide from it."

"Nick," she pointed out, "this could be what *made* everyone vanish. And if we check it out, we could vanish, too."

"Well, at least we'd get an answer, then." He backed away from the window, and confronted her. "I'm going." He paused then, considering. "You could always stay here, you know. Until I get back." He gave her a pointed look.

She sighed. "I guess I'm coming, then." She didn't want to, but Nick was right. They *had* to discover the truth of the mystery. Whatever the "truth" turned out to be. She grabbed her jeans and T-shirt and pulled them on over her pajamas. Then she slipped her shoes on. Nick did the same. Then they headed for the door, as quietly as they could. If there was someone—or *something*—moving in Central Park, then there could be more of the same all over.

Nick led them down to the lobby and out into the street, checking carefully as they advanced. There was no sign of any activity. No noise, no shouting, no nothing. "C'mon," he said. They crossed the street and entered the park. Through the dense stand of trees in the distance they could see the light moving in and out, but Skye couldn't tell how far away it was. Nick started to crawl forward, and Skye grabbed at him.

"No, Nick."

"It's okay," he assured her.

As they came upon the mysterious light Nick slowed down. Skye stuck tight by his side. The trees thinned out up ahead and opened onto a small rolling field. Both of them crouched low for a better view.

There were two figures. It was hard to be sure exactly *who* or *what* they might be. But both of them had heavy-duty lights strapped to their helmets. They wore some kind of space suit as far as Nick could tell—big, yellowish, and very bulky.

"They *look* human," whispered Nick. Skye nodded. Both figures walked on two legs, and were equipped with two arms and a head. But nothing of the their details or physical characteristics was visible. The faceplates of the helmets were a shiny polished black. Each suit had several hose connectors running from large packs they wore on their backs.

One of the figures reached up to a low branch and, with a long tool, snipped off a twig. It then placed the twig into a small pouch, sealed it, and slid it into the backpack. Then it moved on, taking a second sample from a bush.

The other figure had something that looked like a metal detector, and it was fanning this tool back and forth across the ground. Periodically the figure would interrupt this activity to consult a meter or some such tool it carried on its belt.

Close encounters of the worst kind, Skye thought. She was shivering, despite the warmth of the night. Those creatures couldn't be human.

Nick tapped her arm gently, but she still jumped. He nodded back the way they had come, and started off. She followed, thinking with relief that he was going back to the hotel. But he wasn't; he simply wanted to skirt around the two figures and head deeper into the park. They passed one of the ponds and came upon another space-suited figure. It appeared to be taking water samples from the pond. The light from its helmet light glittered eerily off the water.

Skye said: "They *must* be from another planet if they're thinking about drinking Central Park pond scum."

Nick was so surprised by the unexpected comment he had to push a fistful of knuckles into his mouth to keep from laughing.

Skye didn't have any idea what Nick was up to until he gestured ahead of them a short while later. She saw something that made her stiffen in shock.

It was like a hole in the air, as if someone had taken hold of reality and ripped it apart. There was a ragged blackness at the edge of the tear, and towards the center what looked like a tunnel of light leading . . . where? Skye suddenly felt lightheaded and turned her gaze away. That was when she saw two of the figures approaching. She tapped Nick and they both flattened themselves in the closest outcropping of rocks. With her splayed fingers glued to the cold stone, Skye breathed in short, shallow gasps.

"Oh my god," she whimpered. She looked over at Nick, whose face had gone as pale as a ghost.

The two figures approached the ''tear'' and stepped inside it! They plodded down the tunnel until they were lost in the light. A moment later, two more of the figures approached the tear, and walked through.

Skye stared at the light as if in a trance. Then, just as quick as the blink of an eye, it was gone. There was just the bouncing, hovering afterglow produced in her eyes. The hole and tunnel had simply vanished.

Nick was gripping her arm tightly. Skye winced but didn't say anything; the pain proved she wasn't dreaming, at least.

''Aliens,'' she said. ''It's got to be aliens. There's no other explanation for what we just saw.''

''Maybe,'' said Nick. Almost as an afterthought, he finally released his death grip on her arm.

''Thanks,'' she deadpanned. ''And what do you mean *maybe*?'' Without the eerie intensity of the mystery light, he was just a darker shadow in the gloom.

''I just mean maybe. We can't be certain of anything.''

''What's wrong with you?'' she snapped irritably. ''Isn't it obvious?''

''*Is* it?'' he countered. For some reason Skye found his objectivity maddening. ''Anyway, let's discuss this on the way back to bed. I don't think there's anything more to see tonight.''

On that, at least, they agreed. As they started back carefully down the dark path, Skye couldn't help a small giggle. ''Well, at least we don't have to worry about muggers or rapists hiding in the park for once,'' she commented.

"That's true," Nick agreed. "So all you have to watch out for is tripping over something. So—why do you think it has to be aliens?"

"They were wearing *space suits,*" Skye said. "If they were human, they wouldn't need space suits, would they?"

"Not if they *were* space suits," Nick objected. "They could have been biological contamination suits. Maybe there's a lethal virus on the loose that kills all animal life. They'd have to be protected against it."

"We're not," Skye pointed out.

"Maybe we're immune."

She looked skeptical. "If everybody and everything died from a disease, then shouldn't we be up to our armpits in rotting corpses?"

"Not necessarily," Nick suggested. "It could be something like that flesh-eating disease that was in the news. The virus or whatever could have eaten their victims."

Skye shook her head, rejecting the idea. "Aside from the gross-out aspect of what you just suggested, it wouldn't work like that. Even the flesh-eating bacteria doesn't eat *everything*. It leaves bones and such behind. And a terrible stench. The only smell around here is from your socks."

"Ha ha," mugged Nick. But Skye thought he looked a bit put out. Like most boys, Skye thought, Nick hated to be contradicted by a girl.

Nick improvised on his theory: "It could be a new mutant form of the disease," he suggested. "One that eats *everything*."

"You're getting outside of the realm of science and into

magic now,'' said Skye. Nick frowned as Skye sketched out her thoughts: ''Let's just assume for the moment that there *is* such a bug, and we're somehow or other not on its menu. If it *could* eat its victims, then what? If anything eats anything else, there's some sort of leftovers. Even bacteria have to go potty. There should be *some* sort of mess left behind. And anyway, if they *did* eat everything, then there would be no other food left for them, and they'd die, too. In pretty big clumps, so we'd see some sort of remains, I'm sure. Maybe just like a soap scum, but there would be *something*. Sorry, Nick, but I just can't buy the disease aspect.''

''Okay,'' he conceded, ''let's suppose you're right.'' Then, unwisely as it turned out, he outlined another possible scenario. ''What if we weren't exactly immune to the disease, and we just went into a coma or something for several days and then woke up. In that time, the other survivors could have taken all the corpses away and cleaned up.''

Skye couldn't believe him. ''Nick, I think you're seriously overtired. Think about what you just said. Not only would these other survivors had to have removed and disposed of millions of bodies without leaving the slightest bit of mess, but they would have had to have known we were alive. Otherwise we'd have been buried, or cremated, or whatever. And if they knew we were alive, why leave us?''

Nick asked grumpily: ''I suppose you have a better theory?''

''Probably not,'' she admitted. ''But at the very least it's no worse than yours. I think it's obvious that aliens are behind this. Those creatures in space suits were taking samples of life forms that exist here. And that bizarre tunnel isn't like anything that any human engineer would have cooked up. More than likely if this were any kind of biological catastrophe the area would be swarming with medical personnel and sophisticated equipment and stuff." It was too dark for Skye to register Nick's reaction, but she interpreted his prolonged silence as a kind of concession that maybe she was right. She decided not to gloat. "Like I said, it's just a theory."

Tight-lipped, Nick walked on ahead and kicked angrily at a can on the sidewalk and sent it clattering down the street. Skye started to giggle.

Nick turned around to face her. "What's so funny?"

"You," she said. "You're pouting."

Nick curled his lip. "Am not."

"You are, too!" She walked up and took his hand and gave it a squeeze. "Don't worry, Nick. I still think you're the bravest and smartest boy around."

He looked at her with a silent *and?*—then gave her a comic leer. "*And* the cutest?" he prompted.

Skye scoffed. "Don't push your luck, Romeo. And anyway, you're the *only* boy around."

Nick laughed and sang out: "Beggars can't be choosers!" He brought his arms in into a curled position in front of him with fist flat against fist and pantomimed a hulking body builder's pose. "Yaaaaaahhhhh!" he growled. "I am Ahnold!"

Skye burst out laughing. ''You're insane. That's who you are.''

''Speaking of insane,'' he said, returning to his normal voice. ''Let's talk about that theory of yours for a minute.'' They crossed the street on the way back to the Plaza. ''How do you explain that tunnel of light.''

Skye shook her head.

They entered the hotel.

''Maybe it's something that the army developed. Something top secret.''

''Maybe,'' she agreed, not at all convinced. ''Who knows? But I still think aliens are more likely.''

''At least we have something to go on now,'' Nick said. ''Not much, it's true, but something. There is some sort of intelligence involved in all of this. Maybe human, maybe alien. But those space-suited creeps *have* to have some idea what's going on. Which means that we can find out from them.''

By the time they reached their room Skye was feeling wide-awake, wired. But she knew she needed more sleep— if she could sleep after all of this. She peeled off her clothes and hopped back into her bed, pulling up the covers. She talked to the ceiling. ''I have the oddest feeling that, whatever or whoever they are, they aren't likely to just tell us.''

Nick slipped into his own bed. ''Maybe they don't know that anyone is still alive.''

Skye turned to look at him. ''You could hear my music over half the city. They'd have to be deaf not to know we're somewhere around. Besides, the only good reason I can think of for those creeps doing their testing at three in the morning is because they didn't want us to know that *they* were around. They're hiding from us, for whatever reason. And that doesn't make me feel very good about them.''

Nick considered her point. ''There could be other explanations,'' he said. ''But I can't think of one that works. You've got to be right—they're trying to hide from us.''

Skye was surprised. ''Hallelujah!'' she exclaimed. ''You actually agreed with me on something.''

''Don't let it go to your head,'' said Nick. ''It's not likely to happen again in the near future.''

''Probably not.'' Skye smiled to herself. ''Good night. Or good morning. See you at breakfast.''

''Yeah.''

Skye settled down to sleep. It wasn't easy, even though she was bone weary and totally exhausted. There was so much to think about. Her brain was racing a mile a minute. Images flashed through her mind like slides in a projector. The strange characters they'd seen, and their odd experiments. The mystery of the vanished people—and their own immunity . . . It was just too much to take in. There was only one thing she was sure of: she liked Nick a lot. True, he had a fragile ego. He didn't like to be contradicted. But at least he seemed to respect her opinions. And he didn't make fun of her. Most of all he hadn't turned against her— especially when she had needed him most. He had been patient with her, and very understanding.

But for how long? She wondered suddenly. Skye felt the tight fist knotting in her stomach as the odd tormenting fears returned.

What if others turned up. Would he stick with her then? Or would he go with someone else, somebody he liked better? Her throat constricted, and she had a momentary panic attack. She couldn't face the thought of losing him, too. "Breathe, Skye," she told herself. She forced herself to calm down. There were enough bad things in her life already; she didn't have to invent fresh ones for herself. All she could do was to take everything as it happened, and just pray that they would somehow turn out well . . .

Yeah. Right . . .

She waited impatiently for Nick to fall asleep and begin snoring.

It was taking forever.

CHAPTER 7

THE ARGUMENT RESUMED the next morning, and they were still butting heads when they reached the Empire State Building. Nick refused to allow that aliens were behind the disappearances. Skye on the other hand, couldn't accept that humans might be involved. The more they argued the less willing each became to compromise. Nick and Skye kept trying to score points off one another.

"I could buy aliens," said Nick, "if they looked more . . . well, *alien*. But those guys we saw looked like people in space suits."

"And what's wrong with that?" Skye demanded. "If they evolved on a planet like Earth, with the same sort of gravity and conditions, they might well turn out pretty hu-

man. Except for breathing a different atmosphere. Who
says evolution has to take alternative paths? I don't have
any problem with it.''

But Nick, of course, did. To his surprise, he wasn't an-
noyed with Skye for refusing to see his point of view. In
fact, in a weird way he had come to enjoy their arguing.
He even admired her opinions. They were logical and clear.
Then he realized: as long as they were arguing they weren't
thinking how lonely and scared they were.

As she set up the music for the day, Skye couldn't resist
adding: ''And that tunnel. Surely nobody on Earth could
keep something like *that* hidden away forever? It's got to
be an alien gizmo.''

''Are you kidding?'' Nick laughed. ''The military is so
paranoid, they'd keep toilet seats on the top-secret list if
they could. Besides, it might be a really new breakthrough
that we just don't know about yet. Anyway, what do you
think it is?''

''It's obviously some sort of tunnel in space,'' she answered. ''Maybe a quantum singularity or something that's
controllable. It leads from here to . . . wherever those characters came from. And it can be turned on and off somehow. It's fascinating.''

Singu*who*? thought Nick. Whew. Nick had no idea what
she meant by the phrase and he had no intention of asking
for an explanation. Physics wasn't his best subject, and he
knew he wouldn't understand anything she said. But he was
impressed that she was so smart.

Nick noted also that she wasn't as terrified of losing him

as she had been. Maybe the fact that he hadn't vanished overnight had helped. But she'd let him get out of her sight twice this morning already without screaming. Nick had to admit that he was starting to become quite fond of Skye. If they were, for whatever reason, the last two people in the world, he had to admire the taste of whoever or whatever forces had thrown the two of them together.

And she didn't seem to find him totally repulsive, either.

Maybe repopulating the Earth could get quite interesting . . .

And then a flicker of motion caught his eye. He whirled around and saw there was a car driving down Fifth Avenue toward them.

Skye spotted it at almost the same second. "People!" she yelled, and started jumping up and down and waving her hands. Nick was stunned and pleased: there *were* others left, after all! He joined Skye, waving and yelling.

It was a Rambler, and as it drew closer, the driver sounded the horn. Nick could make out two people inside. It stopped a few feet away from them, and both doors opened simultaneously.

The boy who clambered out of the driver's seat looked slightly older than Nick. He had long, dark hair, tied back in a ponytail, and wore a T-shirt and jeans. He grinned and held out his hand. "Thomas Berinsky," he said cheerily. Nick introduced himself and Skye, shaking Thomas's hand.

The girl on the other side of the Rambler was grinning just as widely. She, too, looked slightly older than Nick and Skye, with a mane of blond hair and ice blue eyes. "Chrissie Harmon," she introduced herself.

Nick could hardly believe it. He'd been hoping for more people, but had almost decided that there wouldn't be any others. This was incredible, and they spent the next couple of hours telling each other their stories.

Thomas had been a freshman at Yale, home for a few days in Rye in upstate New York. He, too, had woken to find nobody about, and had set off for the city. On the way he'd run across Chrissie, almost literally. She'd been riding a bike down the Cross Bronx Expressway, and Thomas had been so surprised to see anyone, he'd almost run her down. They'd spent the night in a motel, and started out for the city early, hoping to find other survivors.

Both of them listened carefully to Skye and then Nick as they related their stories. Thomas frowned darkly when Nick explained about the "visitors" in Central Park. He and Chrissie peppered Nick and Skye with questions.

"Interesting," Thomas said at last. "I only wish I had been there myself."

Nick bristled. "I'm not lying," he said.

Thomas gave him a condescending smile. "No, of course you're not. But what we need is more information."

Chrissie agreed. "Do you think they'll be back tonight?"

"I don't know," Nick confessed. "But we could check and see. We both got the impression that whatever it was they were doing they weren't finished."

"We can get up at three and see what's happening," Skye suggested. "They were really obvious last night, so we should be able to spot them without a problem."

"Great." Thomas shook his head. "You guys had all

the fun yesterday, it seems. This is amazing.''

The rest of the day went quite fast. Nick found himself growing a little wary of Thomas. The other boy was two years older than he, and a Yale student at that. He gave the impression that he was just a bit superior to everyone else. Also, he seemed to want to take charge, and Nick wasn't overly happy with that. He and Skye had started this going, and Thomas was a latecomer. He didn't have any business being in charge. On the other hand, he *was* older, and seemed to be almost as smart as Skye.

And that was the other thing that bugged him. Skye was very friendly with the new boy. Nick knew that girls tended to like older boys, and he felt both resentment and jealous. Did he have any reason to be jealous, though? After all, Skye wasn't his girlfriend, or anything; they had just met. He had no business feeling possessive. But he did feel that way.

Chrissie was nice, but in an older sister kind of way. Probably because she was two years older than Nick. It didn't seem fair: how come older girls weren't attracted to younger guys? Nick had the impression that Chrissie merely tolerated him. He felt as if he was being increasingly edged out of things, pushed to the side like a bratty five-year-old.

Then Skye suggested that Thomas and Chrissie join them at the Plaza. ''They're great rooms,'' she said, with enthusiasm. ''And it's close to Central Park.''

''I've always wanted to live in the lap of luxury,'' Chrissie said, with a big smile. ''It's just a shame there isn't any room service, though. That would make it almost perfect.''

"Yeah,'' Thomas agreed. "If you add in big screen TV's and pizza delivery.''

Skye looked doubtful. "I can cook, but I don't think I could manage a pizza yet. Not on a camping stove, at any rate.''

Thomas shrugged. "A lot of these fancy hotels have emergency generators,'' he said. "Maybe we can try and find the Plaza's, if they have one. If we could get the power running for a bit, it would be a great help.''

Cripes, thought Nick angrily. *Why hadn't I thought of that.* He did a slow burn when Skye gave Thomas a "my hero'' smile.

Nick decided he'd better say something, and not look like he had nothing to contribute. "Well, now there's four of us, we can split chores. A couple stay here, and the other two scavenge and try and fix things.''

"Right,'' Thomas agreed. "So, what do you say? The girls get to sit around and relax while we do all the work?''

"Oh, you poor things!'' Chrissie mocked. "Treating us like princesses. Hey, I could live with that.''

Skye shrugged. "I like to work. Besides . . .'' She glanced at Nick. "The two of us are kind of a team. We work well together. Unless you'd rather work with Thomas,'' she added hastily.

Nick blushed clear down to his toes. "No,'' he said in a serious voice, trying to mask his giddiness. "I think you're right; we're a great team.''

Chrissie grabbed Thomas's hand and squeezed it. "And

I'm still milking his guilt about almost running me down," she confessed. "So I'd sooner stick with him. Anyway, let's leave the work for tomorrow, and just get to know one another today." She laughed. "But maybe us girls can go shopping later."

"You're on," Skye agreed.

"Clothing," Thomas said in a loud, eye-rolling whisper to Nick. "Even with only us two guys around, they *have* to look their best to impress us." He winked. "Not that I'm complaining, heh, heh."

Nick made a smirking face. What a colossal dork, he thought. Thomas thought he was *such* a stud.

Despite Nick's bad impression of Thomas, the newcomers turned out to be quite fun. Chrissie and Skye started chattering on about some sorts of girl things, and then went off to look for clothes and whatever, leaving Nick and Thomas together to keep a look out for any further arrivals.

"Do you think anyone else will come?" Nick asked Thomas.

Thomas shrugged. "It's hard to say. I would figure that anyone who might head here should live within a couple of days' journey. Otherwise, they'd head for other places, like Washington, or maybe Boston. If nobody shows up in the next few days, it might be worth our while to travel on down to Washington, actually. It is the nation's capital, and a lot of survivors might gather there."

Nick shrugged. "Yeah, I guess. But it's more important to check on our nocturnal visitors, I think."

"I agree." Thomas yawned. "I sure do hate missing out on my sleep, though."

"No need for you to come along," Nick said. "I can take care of it."

"Thanks," said Thomas, though he didn't sound grateful. "But I think I'd better come along. I'm sure you'll need my help." He chewed at his lower lip for a moment. "My plan is to confront one of these intruders."

Plan? thought Nick, alarmed. Nobody said anything about a plan. Nick asked: "Are you sure that's wise. After all, if they're responsible for the disappearances, confronting them might get us into even worse trouble."

Thomas gave Nick a long suffering look. "What do you say you let me worry about that, okay?"

Nick asked angrily, "But—"

"Look," said Thomas impatiently. "It's the best way to learn what's going on. Do they know that anybody's still alive here?"

"They must," Nick said. "Why else work at night?"

"I don't know," admitted Thomas. "But that doesn't mean that they may not have a reason. Maybe sunlight affects them or something."

"What?" Nick scoffed. "You think they're vampires?"

"Not as such, no," Thomas answered. He saw the bemused look on Nick's face and blurted, "But it would explain what happened to everybody, wouldn't it? A plague of vampires bit everyone and turned the human race into vampires. They either had to hide or burn up in the sunlight. Either way, they're gone. Only we're immune somehow."

Nick counted one, two, three, then said: "You're joking, right?"

Thomas laughed uncertainly. "Uh, of course, my man. I was just pulling your leg. Know what I mean?"

Nick thought, *what a jerk*.

The girls came back with a cart loaded with bags. "It's not all clothing!" Chrissie protested before either of them could say anything. "We scavenged food, and some useful items, too." She opened one bag and pulled out an old-fashioned alarm clock. "Wind-up," she explained. "Perfect for making sure we wake up on time. We found a batch of them in an antique store."

"Great." Thomas glanced at the sky. "Well, guy and gals, it's getting late. Shall we give LeAnn Rimes a break for the night and go off to feast? And an early bedtime, so we'll be functional at three?"

He was taking charge again. Nick couldn't help resenting it. It had almost been better when he and Skye were alone. She seemed to sense his mood and gave his hand a gentle squeeze. That made him feel a bit better.

They all helped to fix dinner, though Nick did all the noncooking parts like setting the table and getting the drinks ready. They all had quite an appetite, and the food was pretty good. Nick thought that he and Skye did better on their own, but he didn't want to antagonize anyone by saying so. After they'd eaten, they carted the rest of the supplies upstairs.

Outside the room, Skye hesitated. "Nick, I think I'd better share a room with Chrissie now." She blushed. "It's more . . . you know."

"I know." Even though he'd been kind of uncomfortable the previous night, Nick was disappointed. It had been nice having Skye so close. It made him feel safe. But he knew she was right. Anyway, she'd only shared the room with him for company, after all, and it was better that the two girls share now. "Anything to avoid hearing me snore," he joked.

"It's not that," Skye said softly. She touched his cheek and then gently kissed him. "I like you an awful lot, Nick. I really do."

"Likewise," he answered, feeling both giddy and terrified.

She grinned. "And you don't have to watch me brush my teeth now."

"They're nice teeth," said Nick lamely. He groaned inwardly. He decided to quickly change the subject. "Which of us is moving out? Me, I guess—I've got less stuff. Especially now."

The four of them moved things around. Thomas didn't offer to share with Nick, which was fine with him. Probably not enough room for him and his king-sized ego, anyway. Nick took a room next to the girls. Thomas chose one several doors down, and said good night.

As Nick got ready for bed, he felt a twinge of loneliness. Maybe Skye's problem was catching. He found he missed having her around. It was odd, since he'd felt so uncomfortable the previous night. But he realized that he was both getting used to her and getting very fond of her. If this were the world the way it had been, he'd definitely have been asking her for a date. If he could have built up the courage! Why would a girl as pretty as Skye ever have looked at a guy like him?

He changed into his pajamas and wound and set the alarm clock for two-thirty. He aimed to be ready for the hunt. Just as he was about to get into bed, there was a soft knock at his door. His heart skipped a beat. It was Skye. She was dressed in her pajamas and was looking slightly embarrassed.

"I just wanted to say good night," she explained awkwardly.

"Thanks."

His mouth was suddenly so dry he couldn't swallow. Skye waited on the landing. She seemed to be expecting something. Nick's heart was pounding so hard he could feel it in his ears. He leaned forward and kissed her. It seemed to have been the right thing, because she grabbed him hard and kissed him back. Nick felt his knees buckle.

Then she broke it off, and looked at him with a different expression. "You're very special, Nick," she murmured.

"Yeah," he squeeked. "Umm. You're really something, too, Skye." Bells were going off in his head. He felt sick to his stomach, and he realized he had never been happier in his life.

Skye nodded, and turned away. He watched her pad back to their old room and sighed as he closed the door.

Sliding under the covers, Nick turned off the flashlight he'd been using for light, and the room was plunged into absolute darkness. And the only sounds he could hear were the pounding of his heart and the rustle of his own breathing.

He missed Skye.

Maybe being lonely *was* contagious . . .

Somehow, despite his twisted thoughts and emotions, he fell asleep. He was having a horrible dream when the alarm clock crashed through his sleep. Nick jackknifed in bed and managed to drop kick the offending clock into silence again. Yawning and scratching, he climbed out of bed and edged up to the window.

There was light in the park again. The intruders were back. This woke him completely, and he hurriedly dressed and grabbed his flashlight. He was the first out. Skye emerged from her room a moment later. She grabbed him and gave him a hug.

"I missed you," she told him.

"Me, too," he replied.

Chrissie emerged next, yawning, and finally Thomas. He hadn't been joking when he said he liked his sleep. He looked like he was walking in it. But it meant that he didn't object when Nick took the lead. And Nick didn't object when Skye took his hand. It felt better holding on to her again.

They went quickly and silently out of the hotel and across the road to the park. Nick guided them through the twisting shadows towards the light, and stopped. Nick looked back over his shoulder. He grinned when he saw Thomas. The older boy looked a lot less confident than the day before. "This way," Nick said.

He stole stealthily toward the lake.

Whatever was happening, tonight the four of them would find out the truth. Whatever it took . . .

CHAPTER 8

SKYE SCANNED ALL about them as they moved through the park. She felt excitement and apprehension in about equal measures. Now that they were four strong, perhaps they could find some answers to what had happened to their world. She was really glad that Chrissie and Thomas had shown up. She liked having another girl around to talk with. Nick wasn't as happy, she could tell, mostly because Thomas had slipped into taking the lead, and Nick resented it. Skye was careful to make Nick realize that she was supporting him.

Besides, it felt good to squeeze his hand, hug him, and give him quick kisses.

Her panic at being left alone was subsiding now. Having two extra people about had helped her a lot. The fear wasn't as great now, and it was as if a suffocating load had been taken off her shoulders and head. She could breathe freely and think clearly once more.

And hopefully, they would soon have some answers that they desperately needed.

The night was dark, with a slender crescent moon often hidden by clouds. The only light was that produced by the strange intruders in the park. But that was enough for the four of them to generally see where they were going well enough.

Thomas had found a second wind and had taken the lead, irritating Nick, and the rest followed him. Flitting from shadow to shadow, they drew closer to the lake. The last stage was taken very slowly, and then they all peered out at what was happening.

There were two of them, both dressed in the same bulky suits. One was taking water samples and slipping the vials into a large refrigerated container. Skye felt a twinge of doubt when she realized that it did indeed look very like a human artifact, one that might be found in a terrestrial laboratory. Maybe Nick was right. Maybe they were human? Or was it just that the similar needs tended to produce similar designs? The other creature was clipping samples from various bushes, and placing these into what looked like plastic specimin bags. These were then stored in its backpack.

It *did* look awfully like human scientists at work. But if that was the case, why the space suits? Surely if the four of them could breathe the air with impunity, anyone could?

Or was it possible that Nick was right and there was some sort of killer virus on the loose that the four of them just happened to be resistant to? Wasn't that asking a whole lot? Especially since, of all the people in the area, the only four who were immune happened to be two couples of virtually the same age.

No. Nick couldn't be right here. This had to be something some bizarre alien race had planned and was carrying out. It didn't make any sense otherwise.

"Amazing," Thomas murmured softly. "This really is incredible. And you're right—whoever is down there *has* to know what's happened."

"So what do we do now?" asked Chrissie.

"Confront one of them," Thomas decided. "We have to ask questions."

"That could get us in real trouble," Nick objected. "What if they don't know we're here? Confronting them would alert them. They could come hunting us next."

"I don't see how they couldn't know we were here," Thomas answered. "That music blasting out every day is a dead giveaway. I mean, we haven't exactly been hiding away."

Nick shook his head. "If they knew we were here, why would they leave us alone?" he complained. "Wouldn't they want to talk to us, examine us, find out how come we're immune?"

"I don't know," Thomas said, exasperation in his tone. "But the only ones who do know are down there. We *have* to get some answers."

Nick considered this, and then looked at Skye. "What do you think?" he asked.

She reached out and squeezed his hand. "I think you're both right," she replied. "And I'm not just trying to stay on the fence. I think we do need to get answers. But I think we need some sort of protection. Maybe we should try and talk to one of them on its own. That way, if there's trouble, we'd be more likely to be able to do something about it."

"That makes sense," Nick agreed.

"Yeah." Chrissie nodded.

"Fine." Thomas looked down toward the lake. The figure who'd been taking the samples was done and was now moving up to the path, probably on its way back to the tunnel, he decided. "How about we ambush that one?"

They all agreed, so they ran back down the path to where they would be out of view of the remaining figure by the lake. Then they waited.

The suited figure finally shambled into view on the path, carrying the sample case and walking slowly. Nick whispered to Skye: "The gear it has on must weigh half a ton. It has to be exhausted." It passed the position where she and Nick were hiding, and approached Thomas and Chrissie.

"Now!" said Thomas, jumping out in front of the figure. Chrissie joined him. Skye and Nick moved to block its retreat.

The figure stopped dead, clearly stunned.

"No!" it said, in perfect English. There was some kind of a radio in the suit. The voice crackled slightly, but it was quite recognizable. "You're supposed to be asleep! This—"

Then he swung the case he was carrying, slamming it hard into Thomas. He grunted and collapsed. The suited figure, however, overbalanced for the contact, and staggered. With a growl, Nick threw himself at it. Skye piled on a moment later, and their combined weight sent the figure sprawling. Chrissie jumped in to help them hold it face down.

"Get off me, you idiots!" it yelled. "You'll ruin everything! Get off!" It struggled to get free, twisting in all directions. Thomas, still having trouble breathing, snarled and jumped down heavily onto its back.

There was a sharp cracking sound. Skye realized that the faceplate on the creature's helmet had been slammed down onto the pavement. There was a terrific yowling cry as the black glass shattered and splintered.

Skye loosened her grip as it struggled, and she fell aside. It turned to her suddenly, and Skye realized she was staring into the face of a human being.

He was screaming, and his face was horribly contorted. He gasped for breath, struggling to his knees, whooping in corrosive lungfuls of air that seemed to burn his throat and nose. He cried out in agony. Nick, Thomas, and Chrissie slid off him and stared in shock as the man clawed for air. His face was going crimson and his eyes bulged painfully.

And then he collapsed.

"Jeez . . ." said Chrissie whispered. She reached gingerly into the helmet and felt at his throat. "No pulse . . . He's dead."

"Dead?" Nick looked as ashen as Skye felt. "But . . . how?"

"I think we'd better keep the questions for later," Thomas said grimly. "Let's get out of here before someone comes looking."

Skye didn't need any further urging. Nick helped her to her feet, and they all walked as quickly as they could back to the hotel. Nobody said a word until they reached the foyer, when Thomas said: "Upstairs!"

They all bundled together in the girls' room. Chrissie was shaking as badly as Skye, and Nick looked pale and disturbed. Thomas, on the other hand, appeared to be more angry than anything.

"They *do* know about us," he said. "And they *are* hiding from us."

"And they're human," Nick said. Skye was glad he didn't give her an I-told-you-so look, but instead took her hand. She hadn't realized how cold she was until it registered that he was a lot warmer than she. She snuggled in close, and he put a protective arm about her.

"Yes," Thomas agreed thoughtfully. "So what gives? And what killed that guy like that?"

"Some sort of bug," Nick stated decisively. "That's why they wear those suits."

"No," Chrissie answered. "I'm in premed, and that wasn't any kind of reaction to a germ, bacteria, or virus. He died of asphyxiation."

"Huh?"

"He couldn't breathe," Chrissie explained. "He choked

to death gasping for air. It's like the air was somehow poisonous to him.''

Skye was bewildered. ''That doesn't make any sense,'' she complained. ''We're not having trouble breathing it. Why should he?''

''I don't know.'' Chrissie leaned wearily against the wall. ''But it's what happened. He died because he couldn't breathe the air that we can.''

There was silence for a moment as they all considered this. Then Nick shook his head. ''Why would perfectly good air kill him? And since we know they know we're here, why haven't they tried to communicate with us?''

''Worse than that,'' Skye pointed out. ''He seemed to be under orders *not* to talk to us. He struggled to get away so we couldn't learn anything.''

''Right,'' Nick agreed. ''That's exactly it.''

''Is this some kind of experiment?'' Thomas ventured. ''One in which we're the rats in the maze?''

''How can it be?'' Chrissie objected. ''I mean, they wouldn't be able to clear out all of New York and the boroughs just to conduct some sort of sadistic test on the four of us, surely?''

''I wouldn't think so,'' Skye agreed. ''On the other hand, I wouldn't think that everyone could just vanish overnight, either.''

''There has to be *some* sense in this somewhere,'' Thomas said firmly. ''Only we just haven't been able to piece it together yet. We need more information.''

Nick gave a very brittle laugh. ''I don't think we're going to find it that simply. That guy was really determined not to talk to us, and I don't think the rest of them will be any different.''

"Plus," Skye pointed out, "when they find his body, the others are bound to suspect that we had something to do with his death.'' She shivered. "After all, we did.''

"Not necessarily,'' Thomas said slowly. "The guy was carrying a heavy load, and he was tired. They might just think he fell over and broke his faceplate when he fell. There's nothing there to incriminate us in any way. And it wasn't our fault he died.''

Skye couldn't help remembering the anger on Thomas's face when he'd attacked the man, but said nothing. He was right, really. The man's death hadn't been anything that they could have possibly expected from what they knew. It was a shock and a shame, but it had truly been an accident.

"On the other hand,'' Thomas added, "it is sort of useful in a way.''

"How do you mean?'' asked Nick.

"We have a weapon now,'' Thomas explained. "If we can get another of those figures alone, we can threaten to smash his faceplate if he won't talk.''

The idea of threatening another human being with a slow and horribly painful death made Skye sick. It was one thing to fight back if you were attacked, but to plan violence seemed abhorrent to her. "I don't like that idea,'' she objected.

"Me neither,'' agreed Nick.

"We don't have to *do* it," Thomas said. "We just have to *threaten* it. It gives us some power over them."

"Maybe," agreed Chrissie, though she didn't sound too convinced either.

"Look, you wusses," Thomas snapped, "it's obvious they're not going to tell us what we need to know if we just ask them pretty please to do so. The one tonight wasn't going to say anything. We *need* to know what's going on, and those goons out there are the only way we can find out. We *have* to do this, as repugnant as it may be. We need the answers, and we're going to have to threaten violence to get them."

Chrissie nodded slowly. "Yeah. I mean, what else could we do if they don't agree to talk? All they have to do is wait, and someone will look for them. And then they know we know about them. Right now they probably think we're totally ignorant."

Skye played with a strand of her hair as she thought about this. Nick gave her a haunted look that she understood completely. This whole thing was getting out of hand. They hadn't been expecting death to be involved. Okay, both of them had to have had the idea that maybe the vanished were actually the dead, but there hadn't been any evidence of this—until now.

Why had that man died? Where was everyone? Why had the four of them been spared? And why were those scientists watching them and not contacting them?

It was no good; she *had* to know. It could literally be a matter of life and death.

"Okay," she decided. "We *threaten*. But if they don't talk, we don't follow through. Agreed?"

"Sure," Thomas said. "We're just after information. I don't want to harm anybody, either. But we *have* to know."

Chrissie and finally Nick both agreed. The four of them sat there, looking at one another for a few silent minutes, and then Chrissie sighed.

"Look, guys, it's really late. Maybe we should all get some sleep."

"If we *can* sleep after that," Nick muttered. But he rubbed his eyes as he said it.

"Right." Thomas stood up. "See you all in the morning. And if they're watching us, we'd better say nothing at all about this until we get back here tomorrow night, okay?" He didn't wait for an answer, but ambled out of the room.

Skye stood up, and Nick held her. "Sleep well," he murmured.

"I hope so," she agreed. She kissed him quickly. "Good night."

Once he had left, she and Chrissie changed back into their nightclothes. Chrissie gave her a hug, and Skye realized that the older girl was as disturbed as she was over what had happened. They both hopped into bed, and Skye tried to settle down to get whatever rest she could.

She kept seeing the poor man's strangled face, bloated and eyes staring. It had been horrible. She shivered and bit back a whimper. Sleep wouldn't be easy—tonight or any other night . . .

CHAPTER 9

NICK WOKE UP feeling terrible. His head hurt, and his conscience hurt him even more. He couldn't forget what he had witnessed the previous night. The dying man's face and choking gasps for breath haunted him. He washed and dressed without enthusiasm, and then went downstairs to wait for the others. Skye was already there, looking as if she'd not been able to sleep at all. Her face was pale, her eyes tortured. He grabbed her and hugged her, feeling her shake against him.

"I'm sorry," she whispered, clutching him tightly. "I can't get that man out of my mind."

"Me neither," Nick admitted. "I've never seen anyone die before. And I hope to God I never do again."

Skye broke free and wiped at her eyes. "You want breakfast?"

"I couldn't keep it down," Nick answered, miserable.

"You two look a sight," Thomas said, joining them. Nick was surprised to see that the other boy was cheerful. "How about some breakfast, while the bacon's still edible?"

Nick shook his head. "No way. Look, I'm going on ahead, okay? I need some fresh air."

"Me, too," Skye agreed hastily. Thomas shrugged, so they left him as he fired up the portable stove to start cooking. Outside, Skye shook her head. "Doesn't it bother him at all?"

"It doesn't look like it," Nick answered. "Maybe he's tougher than we are."

Giving him an odd look, Skye asked: "Is that supposed to be a good thing?"

Nick had to admit that he didn't know. He clutched her hand, and she was grateful. They walked through the silent streets without saying anything. Nick found that just having Skye with him made him feel a little better. It was as if she were taking some of the guilt and pain from him just by being with him. And she seemed to be getting a similar benefit.

"I'm not sure I actually like Thomas," Nick confessed as they drew close to the Empire State Building. "He seems to enjoy being bossy."

Skye looked at him. "Are you sure it's not just jealousy?'' she asked him. ''That he's older than you, and is drifting into taking charge?''

He bristled. He didn't like the idea of being so transparent. Still, she had a point. ''That's a part of it, I guess,'' he confessed, feeling miserable. ''I *am* jealous of him. I was also kind of afraid that you might . . . like him better than you like me.'' He knew his face was red, but he forced himself to keep going. ''Girls like older guys better, don't they?''

''I can't speak for girls in general,'' Skye replied. ''For one thing, there's only one more girl we know of left. But *this* girl likes you better than any other guy in the world.'' She leaned over and kissed him gently.

Nick couldn't believe how good Skye made him feel. But it wasn't just the romantic junk. He found that he could talk to her about things without feeling too weird. ''Thanks for the reality check. But jealousy is only part of it,'' said Nick. ''Thomas is so . . . arrogant. He believes he's right all of the time. And he doesn't seem to have been bothered by that man's death last night. He seems to be the kind of guy I would have always avoided in the past. But we don't have a lot of choice right now, do we?''

''I guess not.'' Skye sighed. ''If it's any consolation, I'm not too happy with him, either. And Chrissie is a bit stuck up, actually. I think she thinks because she's so cute everyone should fawn all over her.''

Nick thought she was looking at him for comment. ''Yeah, she's cute, I guess. But *you're* beautiful, so that means you outrank her.''

Skye laughed, and kissed him again. As she leaned over she tripped on the curb and almost fell. Nick grabbed her, holding her up from falling. He discovered that holding on to her was a rather pleasant feeling.

Skye managed to get her footing and straightened up. "Thanks. I must have . . ." Her voice trailed off as she looked at the curb. "Nick!"

Following her worried gaze, Nick was momentarily confused. The edge of the curb she'd tripped over had powdered to dust, blowing gently away in the breeze. "Wow," he muttered. "That must have been really rotted through or something. It's just crumbled away."

"It can't be," Skye insisted. "It was perfectly fine a moment ago. What caused it to crumble like that?"

This was odd . . . Nick squatted down and touched the edge of the eroded curb. More of the cement broke away and powdered in his hand. "This is mondo bizarre," he decided. "Could something be happening to the cement? Maybe whatever caused the people to disappear? Something that eats away at solid matter somehow?"

Skye shuddered. "All the people turning into dust and blowing away? What a horrible thought . . ."

It was, but it was also one that they had to consider. Just what was happening here? "Is it just this one spot?" Nick mused. "Or is this widespread?"

"We'd better find out." Skye walked to the storefront close by them, and hesitantly reached out toward the brick that supported the window. Her fingers touched the brick . . . and powdered it. She was able to poke a finger several inches into the brick.

This was getting scary. Nick stood beside her and reached his hand out to the glass of the window. He touched it, and it felt normal—slick and solid. Then he pushed.

His hand went through it. It didn't shatter or crack; it simply fell to dust as he pushed. The edges of the hole crumbled as he grabbed at them, the window dissolving at his touch into powder. In the window was a videotape of *The Great Escape*. He grabbed at the box, and as his fingers closed around it, it crumbled to dust.

"Jeez . . ." he whispered, shaking the powder from his hand. "What is going on here?" He was almost afraid to take Skye's hand, in case her flesh started to crumble, too. But she clutched at him for support, and she was as firm, as warm, and as comforting as ever.

"It's as if things are falling apart," she murmured, wide-eyed and clearly scared. "Nick, what could be causing this? I mean, bacteria that can eat flesh is one thing, even if it should have killed us, too. But what could make brick, stone, and glass fall apart like this?"

"Nothing I've ever heard of," he had to confess. "Come on, we'd better get to the Empire State Building and wait for Thomas and Chrissie. Maybe we can get some answers together."

They hurried the last couple of blocks together. Sitting on the sidewalk was their boom box and CDs, where they'd left them the previous night. Nick hesitated, and then crouched down to touch the player. It felt perfectly normal to him. He jabbed at it with a finger, and managed to hurt himself. "Ouch!" he said, grinning. "Well, at least one thing's okay." He put a CD in and started the boom box going. The music helped to relieve some of his panic.

Skye had walked to the building and was touching the doorway. "This isn't crumbling, either," she reported, with a nervous laugh. "So not *everything* is falling apart."

"I suppose we ought to check what is," Nick suggested. "Maybe it was just that one area two blocks up."

It wasn't. It didn't matter which direction they walked, everything they touched that was away from the Empire State Building crumbled if they poked it. They tried everything—stone, brick, glass, metal, cloth, wood. All of it would crumble at their touch.

"This is insane," Nick said, exasperated.

"What is?" Chrissie asked. She and Thomas were approaching, hand in hand. It seemed as if they were getting along just as well as he and Skye.

Between them, Nick and Skye managed to explain. Naturally, neither of the others believed their crazy story until they'd tried it for themselves. After a couple of frantic minutes, the truth of it was evident.

"But this is crazy!" Chrissie exploded, obviously scared. "Why should everything do this?"

"I don't know," Nick admitted. "But only the Empire State Building and everything around it seems immune."

"And the Plaza, obviously," Thomas said. "We touched enough stuff there this morning, and none of that crumbled."

Skye seemed to be hit by a sudden thought. She knelt

down and touched the sidewalk. Her hand penetrated the flagstone, and then she looked startled. "I can only push in about four inches," she reported. "Then it's solid again. But the sidewalk crumbles if you touch it."

"But walking on it doesn't cause a problem," protested Thomas. He looked around wildly. "This doesn't make any sense."

"Hang on," Chrissie said. She ran to where they had left their car from the other day. Nervously she reached out. Her hand pushed through the metal door, leaving dusty remains. "This was perfectly fine the other day," she objected. "Why not now?"

"All of this was perfectly fine the other day," Nick pointed out. "Now look at it!"

"Bloomingdale's!" Skye said urgently. "Come on!" She grabbed Nick's hand and dragged him a few steps, before he could get up to speed and run with her. Chrissie and Thomas followed behind them. They ran in silence until they reached the familiar shop.

Skye reached out and touched the glass in the door. It turned to powder. With a snarl, she jumped at the door. It dissolved as she hit it. Coughing from the dust, she pushed her way inside. Nick followed, and saw her grabbing at clothing, which powdered at her touch.

"This shouldn't happen!" she said angrily. "Look!" She grabbed at a hat, which fell apart.

"So?" Chrissie asked, panting as she arrived.

"So the clothes I'm wearing came from here just two days ago," Skye pointed out. She grabbed at her T-shirt, which simply wrinkled as it should. "How come the clothes we took then are perfectly fine, and the ones we left aren't? If it was something affecting the whole city, why haven't our clothes fallen apart, too?"

Thomas managed a weak grin. "Much as I'd enjoy the sight if they did, I have to admit that you've got a point," he said slowly. "How come only certain things are affected?"

Somehow, things fell into place for Nick. "It's what we've touched and been using," he said slowly. "The Empire State Building, the CDs, the clothes . . . Everything that we *use* is fine. The food and all. But all the stuff we don't touch on a regular basis is falling apart."

"That's dumb," Thomas objected. "Why should that be? It doesn't make any sense."

That angered Nick. "Listen, you idiot!" he yelled. "None of this makes any sense! Why should everyone but the four of us have vanished? What's happening in Central Park? Who are those people we saw? Why are things crumbling? I don't know! But they *are* happening, and we have to live with it. If we can. I can't explain any of it. All I can do is to say it's happening."

"Nick's right," said Skye, intervening quickly as Thomas started to get red-faced. "Only what we've been using is staying real. It's like the rest of everything is just turning to dust somehow."

"But *why*?" complained Chrissie.

Thomas looked grim. "The only ones who know the answer to that one are those jerks in the night," he said grimly. He looked around. "If everything's falling apart, then we have to act quickly. We have to get the answers that we need tonight. There might not be any other time. It's tonight or never." He glared at Nick, as if challenging him to contradict him, but Nick couldn't. Thomas was right.

That night might be their last chance for answers.

None of them could get any sleep. They didn't want to lose their chance or waste time. All through the city, anything that they touched crumbled away to nothing. The only things immune were anything in the Empire State Building or in the Plaza Hotel. Nick had wondered about Central Park, but he hadn't managed to work up the nerve to find out. Nor had any of the others suggested it.

They had all eaten, but none of them had much enthusiasm for it. Skye had huddled next to him for comfort, and he'd been glad of it. Chrissie and Thomas had likewise teamed up and seemed to be better for it. They all needed comfort in this worrying time. Skye felt so wonderful to hold on to, and Nick had to face another reality: he was falling in love with her. Even if everyone he knew were to somehow miraculously reappear, he knew he wouldn't want to lose Skye. She'd gone, over the course of just three days, from a stranger to a pain in the butt to someone he wanted to be with all of the time. She just felt so right for him.

Thomas and Chrissie wandered off together, without a word. Nick was glad. He'd been having trouble with Thomas all along, and it wasn't getting any better. And Chrissie, as Skye had said, was a stuck-up princess. Still, not everyone could be as smart and interesting as Skye . . . He gazed down at her, to find her looking back up at him.

"Nick," she said softly. "I . . ." She swallowed. "This is probably going to scare you, but I have to say it."

"You're actually an alien from Mars?" he said, grinning.

"No, you idiot." She scowled at him. "I think I'm falling in love with you." She looked startled that she'd managed to say it, and hastily added: "I don't want to worry you, or pressure you or anything. But I had to be honest."

"It's okay," he admitted, feeling really good inside. "I was kind of wondering how I could manage to tell you pretty much the same thing."

Skye stared at him almost in disbelief. "You mean that?"

"Yes." He bent down and kissed her. This time she didn't let him up for quite a while. "Well," she murmured. "It's convenient that we both feel the same way."

"Maybe more than convenient," Nick said gently. "What are the odds that, of all the people in the New York area, we two should have been immune to whatever happened to everyone else, be about the same age, and just happen to fall in love with one another?"

"Well, like I said, there isn't a lot of choice, is there?" Skye sighed. "On the other hand, I'm not at all attracted to Thomas. Nor you, apparently, to Chrissie."

"And they are to one another," Nick pointed out. "Two

more people the same age. This can't just be a coincidence. There's something more to this that we don't know.''

''Well, let's pray we get the answers tonight,'' Skye said. ''But there's one thing I know.'' She looked slightly uncomfortable again. ''Nick, I don't want to be alone tonight.''

Nick blushed at the suggestion. It was funny, he thought, that up to this point he would have jumped at the chance to be with a girl as cute as Skye. But it had gone beyond that somehow. He was feeling something just as strong, but deeper. He didn't want to rush things. ''Skye,'' he managed to say. ''I don't think it would be exactly safe for us to share a room again,'' he confessed. ''Not now. Not the way I feel about you.''

''I know,'' she agreed. ''And you're not the only one who feels that way.'' She pulled him in for a kiss again.

It had grown very dark by now, but Nick didn't mind. He pretty much had every feature of Skye's memorized by now. And she was wonderful to the touch . . . Then he realized that he could see her face and hair again.

''The lights,'' he groaned. He glanced out the window to see that there was a glow over Central Park. ''Talk about lousy timing!''

Skye grinned. ''We can pick up where we left off later,'' she promised. ''Right now I think we all want answers more than anything else.''

Nick winced. ''Yes,'' he agreed. ''But it's a close contest.''

''That's how I feel, too.'' She glanced up as Thomas and

Chrissie hurried to join them. "And it looks as if we're not the only ones."

"Come on," Thomas ordered, hurrying for the door. Nick decided not to bother starting an argument now. He and Skye followed the older teens as they hurried across the road to the park.

It took them less than five minutes to find the brilliantly lit tunnel. The space-suited men were just emerging from it, with their specimen bags and cases as usual. The four of them watched from hiding for a few minutes, and Nick gestured.

One of the figures had tried to take a twig sample. The bush was falling to dust where it was touched. This seemed to excite the collectors, who gathered around and conferred for a moment. Then they split up, hurrying as fast as they could in their bulky suits in different directions. Thomas grinned and gestured at one, who was heading into the rocks only a few hundred feet from them.

"Let's go get him, guys," he murmured.

They followed the figure until he was out of sight of the tunnel. It was trying to take samples of the rocks, but they were all turning to dust. Thomas laughed gently, and they split up to surround the busy figure.

"Now!" Thomas called, and they all stepped out to surround the space-suited man. He gave a startled jump and looked around. Realizing he was surrounded, he dropped his collecting bag.

"No!" he exclaimed. "You're not supposed to be here. We can't have contact! It will ruin the experiment . . ."

"Ruin the experiment?" repeated Thomas, angrily. "Come off it. You know what would *really* ruin the experiment? *This* would." He reached into his pocket and pulled out a gun. With a shock, Nick recognized it as the one he and Skye had found two days ago and left in the desk. "Either you talk or I'm going to puncture that suit you've got on. And you *know* what will happen then, don't you?"

"No!" the man begged. "Please! You don't understand!"

"That's the point," Chrissie snapped. "We *don't* understand. And we have to. So talk, or we let you try breathing our air."

"No!" Nick said, horrified. "We can't do that! It would kill him!"

Thomas glared at him. "Listen, jerk-face, we need answers. And *he's* our only source. Either he talks or he dies. It's that simple." He held up the gun. "And don't even think of trying to stop me. This gun's real, and it means that if I shoot you, you'll really die, too. So back off." He held the gun against the space suit. "So, what do you say? Talk or die?"

Nick couldn't believe what Thomas and Chrissie were doing. He and Skye had never agreed to this! But there was nothing either of them could do. Thomas was right—the gun would work on them just as easily as it would on the terrified man in front of them.

"I can't talk," the man said, pleadingly. "It would ruin the experiment if you knew! I can't talk!"

"Suit yourself," Thomas said. "There's plenty more of you." With a nasty smile, he pulled the trigger.

The sound of the gun was almost deafening. Nick cried out as the man howled and collapsed.

CHAPTER 10

"No!"

SKYE WAS shaken by the calm and deliberate violence of Thomas's action. She wanted to throw herself on him and pummel him to the ground, but she knew just how far that would get her. How could he so tranquilly kill someone? She felt sick to her stomach.

Then she realized that Chrissie had moved forward and had fallen to her knees and was shouting something she couldn't understand. Skye was confused. Chrissie was recklessly shredding strips of cloth from her shirt. Suddenly Skye's brain jump-started and she realized that the space-suited man was not dead.

Thomas had shot the man, sure enough—but in the lower leg. Air was hissing from the hole, and Chrissie had wrapped a makeshift tourniquet around the leg just above the hole. As she tightened it, the man seemed to recover slightly. Thomas leaned over him.

"That will stop our atmosphere leaking into your suit too quickly," he said. "Your only hope is to get back to your tunnel, and we won't let you do that unless you tell us precisely what is going on here."

The man's face was barely visible through the dark faceplate, but Skye could just make it out. He nodded. "All right," he agreed, his voice filled with pain that even the electronic distortion couldn't hide. "The experiment's been compromised already, anyway. It can't make things any worse."

Nick moved forward, his fists tightly clenched, his face red with anger. "You maniac!" he hissed at Thomas. "You know Skye and I would never have agreed to this!"

"Which is why we didn't tell you what we planned," Thomas said blandly. "Surely you didn't think these people would just talk because we *asked* them, did you?" He rolled his eyes. "Anyway, this worked, and we're getting what we need to know. So shut up and listen." He turned back to their captive. "So, what's happened to all of the people? And why are the buildings crumbling?"

The man sighed. "Nothing's happened to all the people. They're right where they always were—at home."

"You're lying," Chrissie said flatly. "There's nobody here."

"Because *here* isn't where you think it is," the man answered. He sounded tired. "This isn't New York City. You just *think* it is—and so it is."

Nick frowned. "What are you talking about?"

"This place isn't real," the man answered. "It's a figment of your imaginations. It's whatever you make of it."

"That's crazy talk," Thomas said coldly. "Talk sense, or the next bullet goes through your faceplate."

"I *am* talking sense." The man thought for a moment. "Look, do you have any idea what the Quantum Theory of Matter is?"

"Yes," Skye answered. "Matter is made up of tiny packets of particles, held together by several forces—gravity, electromagnetism, and the strong and weak nuclear forces."

Their captive nodded. "And one of the basic tenets of the theory is that the observer changes the results of an experiment simply by observing it. Well, that's what we've been investigating. The idea of the observer changing the real world. We've been working with people who have psychic abilities. Some of them can do the most amazing things. That tunnel back there," he gestured toward the lake. "It's produced by a team of psychics who can use their minds to overcome any sort of distance barriers. They create a space/time tunnel." He swallowed. "We're actually on a small planet orbiting the star Sirius."

"What?" Thomas stared at him in disgust. "This is New York. I *know*. I've been here often enough."

"It's New York because you *want* it to be New York." The man sighed again. "Look, we created the tunnel with our psychics, but this world we found is uninhabitable by normal humans. The atmosphere is completely toxic to us.

But not to a certain type of psychic. Like the four of you. This world seems to be New York because you *believe* it to be. So it's okay for you. I *know* it isn't New York, and it's lethal to me if I breathe the atmosphere.''

"This doesn't make any kind of sense,'' Chrissie objected.

"The human mind frames the universe,'' the man answered. "Not the other way around. Look, for thousands of years people believed that the Earth was the center of the universe, and the Sun revolved about it. And so it *did*. It wasn't until scientists came up with the theory of the Sun being the center that things changed.''

Skye shook her head. "That's crazy. There are *still* people who believe the Earth is flat—but it isn't.''

"That's because they're outnumbered,'' he answered. "Look, it's not what *everyone* believes that matters. The Earth started revolving about the Sun long before everybody believed in it. There are certain sorts of people—we call them cornerstones—who can alter reality just by thinking about it. Most of them don't know that they have this ability. But they do. If they *believe* something is true, then it *is* true.''

Nick was as bewildered as the rest of them, but his mind was still somehow working. "Then *we're* cornerstones. Is that what you're trying to say?''

"Yes.'' The man nodded. "We have certain psychics who can tell what kind of ability a person has. We used them to find as many cornerstones as possible in the New York area. From them, we selected the four of you as being the most compatible.''

Nick objected. "But how? What about our parents? They would never go along with something like this."

The man snorted disdainfully. "*Parents?* Really. This experiment originated at the highest levels of government. We simply did what we needed to do."

"You bastards," said Skye.

The man shrugged, and resumed his explanation. "Then we drugged your evening meals and when you were completely asleep, you were brought here through the space/time tunnel. It was . . . incredible.

"When we had been here before, this world was a poisonous wilderness, completely devoid of life. Just barren rock and a toxic atmosphere. The moment the four of you came through, all of this appeared. Your minds brought the city into being. We placed you in the duplicates of your room and left you to wake up. Then we began testing the planet.

"At first, everything was fine. You woke up and started to gravitate toward one another. We stayed out of the way, because it was important that you believe this was really your home. We only came out at night to take samples, to see that everything was stable."

"But it isn't," Skye said, dully. "It's falling apart."

"Yes," he admitted. "We couldn't understand it. The first day was perfect—everything was fine. The trees were real, the lakes and everything. The only thing your minds couldn't create was any sort of animal or human life. That exists beyond you. Everything else was fine. But last night we saw that some sort of decay had set in. And today . . . it all seems to be breaking down."

"But what's the *point* of all of this?" Nick cried. "Why are you doing this experiment anyway?"

"To colonize other worlds," the man answered simply. "If we can use cornerstones like you to make hostile worlds habitable, then the whole galaxy is open to us. But we believed it was important that you go on thinking that this was really New York, so that you'd believe in it and maintain it. Only it's obvious that it isn't working. Even though you believed in it, it didn't stay. I can't understand it. It *should* be permanent."

Skye was shaken to her core. If what he was saying was true, then she had an astonishing mental ability that she had never suspected. "But it's all breaking down," she whispered. "Isn't that dangerous?"

"Yes," the man agreed. "So I'm going to call off the experiment. Take you all home again. Return you to your families." He paused. "We will, of course, have to wipe your memories."

"What?" Nick glared at him. "No way!"

"We *have* to," the man insisted. "If you go back to Earth knowing that you have the power to alter reality . . ."

Skye understood. "You're afraid of us," she finished. "Because we're so powerful. We can literally change the world."

"Yes," he agreed thoughtfully. "You *can't* be allowed to remember that."

"No," Nick said coldly. "It's not good enough. If you wipe my memories, I won't be able to remember Skye. And I won't agree to it."

Skye felt a wonderful warmth at his words. It was how she felt, too, and it was terrific to know Nick was just as certain.

"You don't have any choice," the man protested. "You have to come back with us. This world is falling apart. If you stay here, you'll die."

"And if we come with you," Skye pointed out, "we'll lose each other. No, I agree with Nick—that's not an option."

"Look around you," the man said, urgently. "Can't you see what's happening? You're starting to discover the truth, that this is all an illusion. And *it's ceasing to exist!*"

Skye looked up in alarm, and saw that he was telling the truth. The rocks were fading away, the grass vanishing. The sky was lightening, but to a peculiar shade of purple. She coughed, feeling an acrid taste in the back of her throat. The *real* atmosphere—the poisonous one.

Thomas coughed, and the gun fell from his fingers. It vanished before it could hit the ground.

The man was telling the truth! Incredible as it sounded, it was the truth. This place existed only as long as they believed in it.

And they no longer believed in it.

Nick grabbed her shoulder. "Skye!" he pleaded, clearly as scared and sick as she was. "We *can* breathe! We *can!* Believe in it! Believe in *me!*"

"It's not real," she protested, coughing again.

"We can *make* it real!" he insisted. "Believe!"

"You're crazy!" Thomas exclaimed, coughing. "We've

got to go, get out of here while we still can! We'll *die* if we stay here!''

"They'll wipe your memories if you go back!'' Nick cried. ''You'll forget your power. You'll forget Chrissie!''

"I'd sooner forget her than die,'' Thomas snarled. He reached down to the man on the ground. ''Come on! Make them take us back!''

"Yes,'' Chrissie agreed, grabbing his other arm. She coughed, too, as the air started to burn her. ''Quickly!'' Ignoring Skye and Nick, the two of them helped the man to hobble away.

Nick looked at Skye, then clutched at her arm. ''Skye, I don't want to lose you!''

She hugged him tight. ''Nor I you,'' she admitted. She coughed. ''But we can't stay here. It's falling apart! Look at it!''

"But we can change it,'' Nick said.

"We changed it already, and it's breaking down!'' Skye was getting frantic. Thomas and Chrissie had already disappeared from view. Soon it would be too late to catch up. ''We've got to go with them.''

"Then we'd lose each other,'' Nick said. ''And I won't do that. Skye, he was *wrong*.''

Skye stared at him, confused. The world was tearing apart around them. The trees had all vanished, and a cold, bitter wind was tearing at her. She coughed again. How long could they stand this? ''What do you mean?''

"I mean it *was* working!'' Nick explained. ''The Empire State Building was fine. So was the Plaza.'' He grabbed her T-shirt. "*This* is real! Don't you see? They screwed up, thinking we could make *everything* real. It was too much of a strain on us. Do you have this low-grade headache, too?"

"Yes," she whispered.

"It's because all of New York was too much for us!" Nick grinned at her. "We *can* remake reality, but just not that complicated! We need something simpler!"

"Simpler?" Skye stared at Nick. She realized that he was right. He *had* to be right. It made sense. They *could* do it, together. Or else they would die.

The world was disappearing around them. Buildings were dissolving into nothingness. The light from the tunnel shone at them from several hundred feet away. Figures crouched at the entrance were gesturing to them. Skye hesitated, pulled first in one direction, then the other. It wasn't too late. They could still go back.

But that meant she'd lose Nick, and that was unacceptable.

He *had* to be right. All she had to do was to *believe* in him. Her mind was in torment. "But what about our families?"

"I'm your family now, Skye. Now . . . and forever."

"I believe," she whispered, forcing herself to mean it. "Nick, I do believe in us. Together we can do anything." The poisonous atmosphere was starting to whirl about them. "But what can we do?"

"We need something small to believe in," he told her urgently, coughing again. "Before we start to believe that this world is real enough to kill us. What can we do? What is small enough for us to make absolutely, solidly real?''

''Oh, God . . .'' she murmured. And then that gave her an idea. ''Believe in *me*,'' she said, firmly. ''We have to believe in one another. And then in something nice and small. Something just for the two of us . . . A garden . . .'' She remembered one of the things in Mrs. Lopez's Bible that she had really loved. The words came back to her, and she said them softly aloud:

''And the Lord God planted a garden in Eden, in the east; and there he put the man he had formed . . .'' She laughed. ''Believe in me, Nick, and believe in the garden!''

''Yes!'' he agreed, holding tightly to her. He kissed her gently, and she enjoyed the touch. She closed her eyes and kissed back.

She *believed* . . .

Her throat stopped hurting, and the hot, burning, swirling wind dropped to a gentle breeze. There was warmth on her bare shoulders, and sunlight. She opened her eyes to see that there were trees and shrubs and grass all around them. The sky was blue, the sun warm, the wind gentle. Nick was holding her tightly, as if he was afraid to let her go.

It had worked! She looked around. It was beautiful. Then Skye looked down and groaned. She blushed crimson, and locked her eyes closed. Nick pulled back, alarmed.

''Skye? What's the matter?''

Eyes still closed, she curled a finger and pointed down. Nick backed up and looked down. Now it was his turn to blush. He swallowed hard. ''Oops. I guess we haven't worked out all the bugs yet.''

They had both forgotten to believe in clothes!

But after a while that didn't matter. All that mattered was that they had each other. As Skye had always dreamed it should be. Laughing, they set of together to explore this strange and beautiful and frightening and terrifying new world.

Their new world.

Epilogue

WHAT IS REALITY? Is it something external to ourselves? Or is it something that we create for ourselves? As if in a dream. Skye and Nick have found their answer to that question. For them, they *are* their world, their reality. But what about the rest of us?

And what about *you*?

Is what you're thinking *right now* real?

Or are you dreaming?

Can you *ever* be sure?

THIS STORY IS OVER.

BUT YOUR JOURNEY INTO

THE OUTER LIMITS™

HAS ONLY BEGUN....

TOR BOOKS

 **Check out these titles from
Award-Winning Young Adult Author**
NEAL SHUSTERMAN

Enter a world where reality takes a U-turn...

MindQuakes: Stories to Shatter Your Brain

"A promising kickoff to the series. Shusterman's mastery of suspense and satirical wit make the ludicrous fathomable and entice readers into suspending their disbelief. He repeatedly interjects plausible and even poignant moments into otherwise bizzare scenarios...[T]his all-too-brief anthology will snare even the most reluctant readers."—*Publishers Weekly*

MindStorms: Stories to Blow Your Mind

MindTwisters: Stories that Play with Your Head

And don't miss these exciting stories from Neal Shusterman:

Scorpion Shards

"A spellbinder."—*Publishers Weekly*

"Readers [will] wish for a sequel to tell more about these interesting and unusual characters."—*School Library Journal*

The Eyes of Kid Midas

"Hypnotically readable!"—*School Library Journal*

Dissidents

"An involving read."—*Booklist*